THE 5 STONES OF DAVID

A TALE FOR DEFEATING LIFE'S GIANTS

KRIS HEAP

Published by Kris Heap

www.krisheap.com

Cover design by Andre (Elevence)

ISBN: 978-0-9836824-5-5

AUTHOR'S NOTE

In writing *The 5 Stones of David*, I set out to honor one of the most iconic and beloved stories in sacred scripture: the rise of a shepherd boy who defeated an unbeatable giant.

As I approached David's story, I did so with reverence for the biblical text. I carefully followed the events as they are recorded in the scriptures and tried to stay true to them as much as possible. At the end of each chapter, I include the verses from the Bible that inspired that section. But like every great tale passed down through time, the Bible leaves spaces between the lines—gaps in the story where imagination must walk hand in hand with faith.

This book is the result of stepping into those gaps. It is not a retelling, but a reimagining. It is what *might* have happened, woven with what we know did. I spent time in the silent spaces where scripture doesn't speak. I thought about David and imagined the fears that were never written, the conversations that shaped him, and the experiences that helped prepare him for his divine destiny. I then repeated that process for King Saul, the prophet Samuel, and the other characters in the story.

Many of the songs and prayers found in the book of Psalms were written by David—the same shepherd, warrior, and king whose story fills these pages. Though we cannot always know exactly when in his life each psalm was penned, their timeless truths reflect the very soul of his journey. At the beginning of each chapter, I've included a verse from one of David's psalms that speaks to the moment—echoing the lessons learned, the battles faced, or the quiet reflections that shaped him.

In that sense, this book belongs to a new kind of genre —perhaps best described as "faith-based historical fiction with a self-help soul." While rooted in ancient history and sacred tradition, it also speaks to the modern reader's heart. Beneath the shepherding and anointing oil are lessons for each of us: how to cultivate vision, summon courage, persevere through trials, prepare with purpose, and live with faith. These are not just David's stones—they are ours too.

As you read David's story, it may help to ask yourself: **What "giant" am I facing in my life right now?** The lessons David learns on his journey are eternal and, just as they strengthened a young shepherd, can strengthen you as well.

May this book inspire you not only to learn of David's story, but to discover your own, as you face the giants in your own life today and in the future.

*"Then he took his staff in his hand, **chose five smooth stones from the stream**, put them in the pouch of his shepherd's bag and, with his sling in his hand, approached the Philistine."*
1 Samuel 17:40

PROLOGUE

Three thousand years ago, a small shepherd boy walked alone onto a battlefield, ready to face the most feared enemy of his time, a giant of epic size and strength. Against all odds—and in the face of certain defeat—he did not falter. Without armor, without experience, and without fear, he stepped forward and achieved the impossible, changing the course of history forever.

How did he do it?

This is his story...

CHAPTER

ONE

THE KING

"You save the humble but bring low
those whose eyes are haughty."
—Psalm 18:27

The sun blazed over the battlefield, its golden rays reflecting off the king's polished armor. The enemy's banners lay trampled in the dust, their warriors scattered or slain. Around him, Israel's soldiers roared in triumph—their voices a song of victory that carried on the wind.

King Saul stood tall in his chariot, the crown glinting on his brow. He raised his sword high, the blade still marked with the blood of his enemies. "The Lord has delivered us!" he shouted, his voice carrying over the tumult. The soldiers answered with cheers, their faces alight with pride and adoration.

This was Saul at his height—the chosen king, the anointed leader of Israel. He had united the tribes, defeated their enemies, and restored the people's faith in their own strength and in the Lord's promises. But as the cheers rose around him, Saul's thoughts were not on the Lord's deliverance, but on the glory of his crown and the magnitude of his victories.

From the edge of the battlefield, Samuel, the prophet of Israel, stood silently watching the scene. His weathered face betrayed no outward emotion, but his eyes lingered on Saul with a thoughtful and solemn expression. The prophet's heart was burdened, for he knew a dangerous secret: the king was losing the Lord's blessing.

Oblivious to that fact, King Saul stood on his chariot, soaking in the people's praise, blind to how far he had already fallen.

A sudden gust of wind stirred the field, lifting dust and the remnants of torn banners into the air. It condensed into a narrow, concentrated whirlwind near Saul's chariot, causing the horses to neigh and rear slightly. Saul turned, frowning as he tightened his grip on the reins. "Steady!" he yelled to the animals with a sharp voice.

Samuel watched the column of dust intently. The movement was unnaturally contained, as though formed by unseen hands into a swirling pillar. The hairs on the back of his neck stood on end, and his heart quickened. It was not the first time he had witnessed such a sign—an omen of warning, a divine message to those who were willing to listen.

The whirlwind hovered ominously in front of Saul for an instant and then dissolved. The king dismissed it with a scoff. "It's just the wind," he said aloud, waving a hand dismissively at the settling dust. His tone carried a hint of irritation, betraying his annoyance that nature itself had dared to disrupt his moment of triumph.

The prophet's lips pressed into a tight line, his eyes troubled. In his heart, he felt the Lord's sorrow, knowing the gust had not been mere coincidence but a rebuke—a warning to the king's increasing pride and disobedience.

Saul dismounted from his chariot, striding toward Samuel with a triumphant smile. "Look, Samuel!" the king said, gesturing to the battlefield. "The Lord has delivered the Amalekites into my hands, just as He promised. The people rejoice, and Israel is victorious once again."

Samuel's eyes shifted to the soldiers, who were herding captured livestock—sheep, oxen, and camels—into makeshift pens. The prophet's face hardened. "You were commanded to destroy everything, Saul, every man, every beast. The Lord said that nothing was to remain."

The king's smile faltered, but only for a heartbeat. He waved a hand dismissively. "This is what the Lord's people want. Am I not called to serve them? Don't worry Samuel, the best of the livestock will be sacrificed to the

Lord as a tribute. Is that not fitting for the God who granted us this victory?"

Samuel turned his eyes from the livestock to address Saul directly, his voice calm but firm. "Obedience is better than sacrifice, Saul. You know this. The Lord was specific that you destroy all the spoils of war. It is not wise to put your own ambitions over the will of the Lord. How many times have I been sent to remind you of this?"

Before Saul could answer, their attention was drawn towards a nearby commotion. Two soldiers were struggling with a man in chains who fought them violently.

Samuel's eyes widened at the sight before turning his attention back to the Saul. "And why is the king of the Amalekites, still alive?" he said with an increasingly firm tone.

Saul's expression changed into a self-assured smirk. "Ah, yes—King Agag. A fine trophy of war, is he not? His capture will send a message to our enemies. The people needed to see their king victorious, not just in battle, but in power."

Samuel was almost stunned into silence by Saul's brazen defiance of the Lord's commands, but he felt something in his heart prompting him to speak. The prophet took a step forward, his voice full of an unseen authority. "Saul, your continued disobedience will be your downfall. I fear you have been rejected by the Lord and your days as king will soon come to an end."

If the king heard Samuel's words, he did not seem affected by them. He was already turning away, calling out orders to his men, his voice filled with the confidence of a man who was convinced he had done what was right.

Samuel remained still, his thoughts swirling like the dust storm he had just seen. He whispered a prayer under his breath, his heart heavy with foreboding.

THAT NIGHT, as the camp celebrated, the prophet Samuel sat alone by the dying embers of the fire. The sounds of laughter and song rang hollow in his ears. He had seen the cracks in Saul's faith, the subtle unraveling of a man who had once trusted the Lord but now only sought glory for himself. And though the wind had stilled, its warning continued to swirl in Samuel's thoughts.

As he sat in silence, the prophet suddenly heard a soft and familiar voice in his mind: "It is enough. I have rejected Saul as king and chosen another—a man after my own heart. Prepare yourself to anoint a new king of Israel."

Samuel was accustomed to receiving guidance from the Lord, but hearing these words caused his heart to sink. Though he had expected this moment was coming, hearing the Lord confirm it caused a deep sorrow to come over him. He stared into the fire, its flickering light reflected in his eyes. "So, the Lord has decided to move on from Saul," he said as his mind started to process the full impact of what that meant.

The demands of the prophet's divine calling were

taxing: so many nights spent alone, praying for a nation lost in its own pride, followed by the burden of delivering truths that nobody wanted to hear. How could he tell the people that the king they had longed for, their champion in battle, the man chosen by the Lord, was now rejected? At the very height of his power and popularity with the people, Saul had lost the blessing of the One who had called him.

A loud crackle from the fire pulled the prophet from his thoughts. He looked up to see the fire shifting unnaturally, its flames twisting into recognizable shapes. Samuel looked more closely, trying to make sense of the forming patterns. In the dancing flames, he could see something: the image of a lone tree on a hillside, a boy resting beneath its branches. The scene remained for a moment, and then the embers shimmered again, changing from one image to another: first into the form of a harp, then a winding road, and then into the towering silhouette of a giant. As the flames began to return to normal, Samuel could see the faint image of a crown falling to the floor. The full meaning of the images was elusive, but the final message was undeniable—Saul had fallen, the time had come to call a new king.

In the distance, Samuel could hear the king's laughter echoing through the camp, loud and unrestrained, the sound of a man unaware that the Lord's favor had begun to slip away and whose days on the throne would soon come to an end. Samuel's heart sank, knowing that in the morning he would have to deliver the Lord's rebuke to the king.

Samuel whispered into the night, his voice carrying both prophecy and regret: "Oh Saul. You were destined for greatness, but your pride has caused you to fall. The crown may rest on your head today, but it is not yours to keep. The Lord has chosen another, and the course of history will change."

Scriptures influencing this chapter:

- 1 Samuel 15:1-3 – The Lord's instructions for Saul
- 1 Samuel 15:13-22 – Saul defeats the Amalekites
- 1 Samuel 15:10-11 – The Lord's rejection of Saul

CHAPTER

TWO

THE SHEPHERD

"He maketh me to lie down in green pastures:
he leadeth me beside the still waters."
—Psalm 23:2

Far away, the same wind that had once stirred the battlefield of Saul's victory now rustled the grass on a hill outside the village of Bethlehem. Beneath the shade of a solitary olive tree, a young boy lifted his head, sensing a shift in the air. He put down the harp he had been carelessly strumming and rose to his feet, his curiosity piqued.

"Wind blowing from the east?" he thought. "That's odd for this time of year."

The hillside was quiet except for the soft bleats of his sheep, grazing in their familiar patterns. David counted them, his gaze sweeping over the flock. All were accounted for, yet his unease lingered. Something about that wind left him unsettled. His mother's voice came to him faintly—a memory from years past: "Winds from the east bring…" But the rest of the words trailed off in his mind, just beyond his reach.

"Perhaps it's time to head back home," he muttered to himself, though the thought brought little comfort.

Home. The word hung heavy in his chest as his mind replayed a scene from earlier that day.

The morning had begun like any other—except that today David would demand to work with his older brothers. He trudged up the slope, his small hands clutching a sickle that seemed too large for him. His heart thudded with nervous excitement. Today, he decided, would be the day he proved himself.

David was young, but he no longer saw himself as a little boy. To his seven older brothers, however, he was nothing more than a nuisance. The oldest were strong and broad-shouldered, their arms weathered from years of hard labor. They worked the fields and tended the family's business in town, roles that David longed to share. Instead, he was given the sheep—the loneliest and least glamorous task in the family.

As he crested the hill, he saw his brothers gathered by the work tent, their deep voices carrying on the wind. Eliab, the eldest, was sharpening a plow blade. Abinadab and Shammah were hauling sacks of grain, their muscles flexing under the weight. The sight filled David with both admiration and yearning. He wanted to stand among them, to be counted as an equal.

Squaring his shoulders, he approached, the sickle clutched tightly in his hands.

"I want to work with you today," he announced, his voice sounding stronger than he felt.

The brothers turned, their faces a mixture of surprise and amusement.

"You want to work with us?" Eliab said, raising an eyebrow. "And what do you think you'll do, David? Carry water buckets? Chase mice out of the grain?"

The others laughed—loud and unkind. David's cheeks burned, but he refused to back down.

"I can do anything you can do," he said, lifting the sickle for emphasis.

"That thing's bigger than you are," Shammah snorted. "You'd hurt yourself before you managed a single row."

David's grip on the sickle tightened.

"I'm not a child anymore. I can learn."

Eliab set down the plow blade and walked over, towering above David. Placing a heavy hand on his younger brother's shoulder, he spoke condescendingly, "Listen, little brother. It's not about learning—it's about strength. You're not ready for this kind of work. Stick to the sheep; they're more your size."

"But I don't want to watch sheep forever!" David blurted out, his voice rising. "I want to do something important, something that matters."

The laughter came again, louder this time. Abinadab

wiped his brow with a calloused hand before responding, "Something that matters? You're a shepherd, David. The only thing that matters in your life is keeping the sheep safe. You always have these ridiculously big ideas in your head. They are going to get you in trouble."

Eliab shook his head, his expression growing serious. "Know your place, David. There is honor in tending sheep. Don't waste your time dreaming of things you'll never do."

David's stomach churned as the words sank in. He looked down at the sickle in his hands, suddenly feeling foolish for bringing it. Their ridicule made him feel smaller than ever.

Without another word, he turned and walked back down the hill, his head low, tears forming in his eyes. The sound of their laughter followed him, each chuckle like a knife twisting in his chest.

David had fled to these hills, his pride battered. Yet, among his sheep, he found some measure of peace. His flock gave him something no one else did—silence without judgment. They listened, never laughing at the dreams his brothers so easily dismissed. But today, even the company of his sheep couldn't erase the ache in his heart.

"They don't understand," he muttered as he thought about his brothers. "To them I'll always be just a foolish child who will never amount to anything."

The sheep wandered closer, their soft bleats filling the silence. David sighed and reached for his sling, slipping a jagged stone into the leather pouch. He swung it idly, sending the stone flying toward a distant tree. It fell short, disappearing in the tall grass.

"I'm not small," he whispered desperately as tears pricked his eyes again. "I just... haven't had a chance to prove myself yet."

He thought of his brothers again—so strong, so sure of their place in the world. He thought of his father, Jesse, who always gave him the smallest tasks. But most importantly, he remembered the stories his mother had told him from a young age about how the Lord had chosen Abraham, Joseph, Moses, and Joshua—not for their strength, but for their faith.

"You don't need to be big to do something big," David said, though he only partially believed his own words as they trailed off into the morning air.

Still, discontent stirred within him as he looked at his sheep.

"Is this really all I'm ever meant to be?" he whispered; his words carried away by the same wind that had unsettled him moments before.

As if summoned by his question, a figure appeared on the path below. An old man—stooped yet steady—led a cow laden with packs. His robes were simple, his beard streaked with silver, and around his neck hung a hollow ram's horn, capped at one end. There was nothing extraordinary about him, yet his presence was like the eastern wind—unexpected and unsettling.

The old man paused and, looking up at the hillside,

raised a hand to beckon David closer. With a mixture of curiosity and caution, David propped his harp against the tree and approached.

"Who are you, young man?" the traveler asked, his piercing gaze fixed on David.

David hesitated. "I am nobody," he replied timidly, lowering his eyes. "Just a shepherd."

"Nobody?" the man echoed, his gaze shifting to the sheep grazing behind David. "Then why has the Maker entrusted you with this flock? Surely a 'nobody' would not be given such a great responsibility."

David's cheeks flushed. "Great responsibility? This is the least important job in my family. My brothers say this is all I'm good for."

"And yet," the man said steadily, "without you, these sheep would scatter. They would fall to hunger, to the elements, to wild beasts. To them, you are everything—the difference between life and death. Does that sound meaningless to you?"

David opened his mouth to argue but paused. Somehow, he had never considered it from the perspective of the sheep.

The old man continued, "If you believe you are meant for something greater, then learn to master what is already in your hands. A shepherd does not merely watch his flock—he leads, he protects, he sacrifices. And sometimes, that is what prepares him for a calling far beyond the hills he has known."

David laughed. "Prepare me? For what? Herding camels?"

The man smiled faintly. "I have known shepherds who were called to leave their own flock to guide another. Even the great Abraham began as a shepherd. Perhaps there is something great waiting for you."

Without another word, the old traveler turned and began walking down the road to Bethlehem, leaving the shepherd to contemplate his words. David watched him for a moment, then called out, "Be careful; there is a strange wind blowing from the east. There might be a storm coming."

The old man paused for a moment, then turned his head and called back, "I think you are right, there is a storm coming. As they say, 'Winds from over the eastern wall bring the traveler fortune or fall.'"

David watched him walk slowly down the road, amused by their brief conversation. As he turned back to his sheep, their bleats somehow sounded a little richer, their presence more significant. He wondered: Was the old man right? Could these rolling hills and long days be shaping him for something he could not yet see?

"Nah," he snorted. "Shepherds don't get to dream."

SCRIPTURES INFLUENCING THIS CHAPTER:

· 1 Samuel 16:1-3 – The Lord's sends Samuel to Bethlehem

"The steps of a good man are ordered
by the Lord: and he delighteth in his way."
—Psalm 37:23

Late afternoon light spilled over the dusty streets of Bethlehem as a messenger arrived, his voice full of urgency. He passed through the gates near Rachel's tomb, pausing only to catch his breath before crying out, "Samuel is coming! Samuel the prophet is on his way!"

The news rippled through the village like a stone dropped in still water. Excitement mixed with unease as neighbors gathered in doorways, whispering to one another. The name Samuel carried weight, evoking both reverence and fear. This was not a man of small renown.

Tales of his fiery judgments and miraculous deeds were legendary. To some, he was "Samuel the Deliverer" to others, "Samuel the Destroyer."

Eliab, the eldest son of Jesse, was in the marketplace when the news reached him. He quickly concluded his business and sought his brothers. He found Abinadab and Shammah at the well, talking with some young women who lingered over their water jars.

"Abinadab, Shammah," Eliab called urgently, "we must go. Now!"

Abinadab turned lazily, a faint smirk on his lips. "What's the hurry, brother? Surely nothing is more pressing than aiding these fine young ladies." He offered a wink, eliciting soft giggles.

Eliab's tone grew sharper. "Samuel the Prophet approaches Bethlehem. He will be at the gates soon."

The smiles vanished. The brothers exchanged quick glances, their casual demeanor replaced by curiosity and concern.

"Samuel?" Shammah asked, his brow furrowing. "Why would he come here?"

"No one knows," Eliab replied. "But Father must be told. We need to hurry."

The brothers bid their farewells and followed Eliab toward home. Along the way, they were slowed by the growing crowd converging near the city gates. The atmosphere was thick with questions and speculation. Was Samuel bringing judgment? A blessing? News from the battlefront?

The three brothers were trying to push through the crowd when Samuel's silhouette appeared on the horizon, etched against the dusty sky. The murmurs ceased as every head turned to watch his approach. He came alone, leading a large cow by a simple rope. His robes were plain, his stride unhurried. There were no banners, no fanfare; yet his presence was commanding.

The Elders of Bethlehem stood at the gate, their faces betraying nervous anticipation. When Samuel was close enough, one of the Elders stepped forward, his voice trembling slightly. "Welcome, Prophet. Do you come in peace?"

Sensing their nervousness, Samuel raised his hand in a gesture of reassurance. "Be at peace. I have come to make a sacrifice to the Lord."

A collective sigh of relief swept through the crowd. Still, questions lingered in the air.

"Why Bethlehem?" another Elder ventured. "Surely the tabernacle in Shiloh would better suit such a purpose."

Samuel's gaze remained steady. "The Lord has sent me to Bethlehem. The reason will soon be revealed."

Before the crowd could press further, a woman's voice rose above the murmurs. "What news do you bring of the war? Our sons fight alongside King Saul, and we have heard nothing."

Samuel's expression softened as he addressed the crowd. "Israel has prevailed against the Amalekites. Their king, Agag, has been taken prisoner."

Cheers erupted, joyful cries filling the air. Mothers embraced one another; fathers clasped hands in relief. Songs of praise to King Saul began to rise.

But Samuel's face did not mirror their excitement. To himself, he muttered, "A victory, yes—and a great loss. The Amalekites' king is defeated, but our own king has fallen."

He turned back to the Elders. "Prepare yourselves for sacrifice. I will offer it at the house of Jesse. Direct me to his home."

At the mention of Jesse's name, Eliab stiffened. "Our father? What could Samuel want with him?"

The crowd parted as Samuel was shown the path leading to Jesse's home. Whispers followed in his wake: "Why Jesse? What could it mean? "

The brothers pushed through and hurried ahead, their minds racing as fast as their feet.

The air was charged with excitement—a rare energy that swept through the village like an unseen force. For in times like these, when shifting winds bring prophets to walk among them, even the smallest of villages might find itself at the crossroads of history.

Scriptures influencing this chapter:

· 1 Samuel 16:4-5 – Samuel arrives in Bethlehem.
· 1 Samuel 17:12-13 – The sons of Jesse named.

FOUR

PREPARATIONS

"No one from the east or the west...
can exalt themselves. It is God who judges:
He brings one down, he exalts another."
—Psalm 75:6–7

The quiet hum of the household was broken by the sound of hurried footsteps. Jesse, seated in a well-worn chair near the hearth, stirred from his light doze. Before he could fully rise, the front door burst open, and his three eldest sons tumbled in, their faces flushed and their breaths heavy.

"Samuel the Prophet is coming!" Eliab exclaimed, his voice brimming with urgency.

Jesse blinked, trying to make sense of the words.

"Coming to Bethlehem? That is...unusual," he said cautiously, rising to his feet.

"No, Father," Abinadab interjected, still catching his breath. "He's coming here—to our house!"

The announcement hit Jesse with unexpected force. He sank back into his chair, his thoughts spinning. "To our home? For what purpose? Did he say?"

"No, only that he's coming to make a sacrifice, and that the Elders of the city are to gather at our house," Shammah replied.

Jesse fell silent, his mind racing through the possible reasons for this unexpected visit. How could Samuel, the great prophet, even know who he was? Prophets do not often visit common people—and yet, he was coming.

"Father!" yelled Abinadab. "What should we do?"

Jesse snapped from his thoughts. "Gather the servants. Call your brothers in from the field. We must prepare quickly."

As Jesse's household sprang into action, Samuel slowly made his way through the bustling streets of Bethlehem. The prophet moved slowly, but with purpose, his thoughts far from the murmurs and stares of the townsfolk who parted reverently before him. His mind was deep in thought about King Saul.

Until a few years ago, Israel had no king. For centuries, the Israelites had been led by prophets and judges who attempted, with mixed results, to follow the Lord. But times had changed, and this generation clamored for a king, yearning to be more like the mighty nations that surrounded them. Despite Samuel's heartfelt pleas to reconsider, the people's cries prevailed, and he was tasked with finding a ruler. But where could he find a man who was strong enough to lead the people yet humble enough to follow the Lord?

Then, in what seemed like nothing short of a miracle, Samuel was led to a young man named Saul. It appeared that God had provided the perfect answer to Israel's cries for a king. Saul stood out as perhaps the most remarkable young man in all Israel—tall and strong, but with a kind and humble spirit that set him apart. If Israel desired a king, the Lord had seemingly delivered one beyond Samuel's greatest hopes.

But despite fitting the perfect image of a king on the outside, Saul dealt with internal anxieties. Timid and even scared to step forward as a leader, he tried to run and hide on the day of his coronation. But Samuel mentored the new king through his self-doubt like a loving father, helping him increase in confidence and faith. Over time, Saul grew into the king that the Lord had called him to be, and Samuel couldn't have been more pleased.

Yet, within a few years, Samuel's hopes had unraveled. As his power grew, Saul began to trust his own strength and wisdom rather than the voice of the Lord. Samuel urged him back time and again, but Saul only drifted further from the man he was called to be. And now Samuel found himself here in Bethlehem, sent by the Lord to anoint a new king to take Saul's place.

"Oh, Saul," Samuel thought sadly, tears forming in his eyes, "you were destined to lead this people to greatness, yet you yourself have fallen. Though you still sit on the throne, your power has faded, and today it will pass to another. How swiftly strength crumbles when untethered from faith. Pride certainly goes before the fall."

SCRIPTURES INFLUENCING THIS CHAPTER:

· 1 Samuel 8:6-22 – The people demand a king.

· 1 Samuel 9:1-2 – Introduction of Saul.

· 1 Samuel 9:15-17 – The Lord confirms that Saul is to be king.

· 1 Samuel 9:21, 10:21-23 – Saul's lack of confidence.

· 1 Samuel 13:8-13 – Samuel warns Saul about not following the Lord's commands.

CHAPTER
FIVE
IN THE PALACE OF THE KING

"Unless the Lord builds the house,
the builders labor in vain."
—Psalm 127:1

Miles away, at the royal palace in Gibeah, Saul sat alone in his chamber, the crown of Israel in his hands. Its cold metal edges bit into his palms, a cruel reminder of the burden it symbolized. The room was dark save for the faint glow of a dying fire, the embers casting restless shadows on the stone walls. The silence pressed in on him, broken only by the uneven rhythm of his breath.

Even as the people were celebrating the victory over the Amalekites, the prophet Samuel had come to him with disturbing news, the words echoing in Saul's mind for what felt like the thousandth time: "The Lord has rejected you as king."

The memory struck like a hammer, each repetition deepening the cracks in his fragile sense of control. How could it be true? Had he not fought for Israel? Had he not defeated their enemies? Had he not built this kingdom with his own hands? He had always obeyed the Lord—or at least he had tried.

His gaze drifted to the sword mounted on the wall, a trophy from his first victory as Israel's king, its blade gleaming faintly in the firelight. He could still hear the cheers, see how the people lifted him onto their shoulders, declaring him the savior of Israel.

But now, the memory soured. Despite the incredible victory, that same battle had ended with the prophet Samuel's reprimand: "You were impatient, Saul. The Lord commanded you to wait and trust in Him, but instead you relied on your own strength and rushed into battle. You must do better next time." Over time, the cheers from the victory had faded, but Samuel's rebuke lingered.

Saul clenched his fists, his knuckles white against the cold metal crown. "The Lord asks too much," he muttered, his voice low but sharp. "No man can meet such impossible demands. If I had waited, my soldiers would have seen me as weak."

As his thoughts swirled, Saul recalled that similar scenes had repeated themselves at almost every battle Israel fought. The king and his advisors would make plans for the battle, and then Samuel would show up with a specific request from the Lord that would seem to change or undermine those plans.

Saul had grown tired of this pattern and, as his victories continued, he decided he no longer needed to listen to the prophet, convincing himself that his success in battle and the praise of the people were signs that he was doing what was right.

But despite Saul's victories, Samuel persisted; each time delivering the Lord's instructions before the battle, followed by prophetic rebuke after. And now the prophet had gone so far as to claim that the Lord was going to replace him as king while at the very height of his strength. It was ridiculous!

Saul pushed himself to his feet, pacing the chamber like a caged animal. His shadow flickered on the walls, becoming larger and more distorted with each step. "Samuel," he spat the name, his voice trembling. "You were supposed to be my guide, my support. But you were always so quick to judge, so slow to forgive. What king could live up to your impossible standards? You called me the Lord's anointed, and yet you stripped me of my power before I could even grow into it."

He paused, his chest heaving. For a moment, his tone softened, almost pleading. "I wanted to do what was right, but you gave me no room to lead. What did you expect of me, Samuel? To let my people falter while I waited for signs from heaven? Am I not enough for you?"

The king's emotions were swirling inside him like a

tempest. But beneath it all, a voice suddenly whispered to his heart:

"You chose this path."

Saul froze, the crown slipping from his hands and clattering onto the stone floor. The sound echoed in the chamber like a loud accusation. He closed his eyes, but the voice persisted, quiet but relentless.

"You chose to act when you were told to wait. You chose to sacrifice when obedience was required. You continually choose your pride over My command."

"No," Saul whispered, his voice cracking. He pressed his hands to his temples, as if he could block out the voice within. "I did what was right. I did what any king would do. The people needed a leader! I gave them strength and victory when Samuel only offered them words."

But the voice would not relent. "And now I must give to another what you have squandered."

Hearing those words, Saul's eyes widened and darted to the shadows that crept along the walls. He could almost see them taking shape—men taller, stronger, and more beloved than he had ever been—coming to take his throne. Perhaps it was one of his own captains, waiting for the right moment to strike. Or a nameless figure in the villages gathering support from the people.

A cold shiver ran down his spine. "What if he's already here? What if the one who will take my place is walking in my kingdom, watching, waiting?" Saul shook his head violently, trying to banish the thought. "No," he declared. "I will crush any threat before it gains power."

His pacing stopped as his gaze fell to the fire, now reduced to a faint glow. The embers sputtered weakly, sending up a final spark before fading into ash. The room plunged into complete darkness as Saul sank back into his chair, the room cloaked in silence. The words Samuel had spoken echoed once more, a ghost haunting his mind: "The Lord has rejected you as king."

He clenched his fists, his voice rising in defiance. "If the Lord has turned against me, then I will rule without Him. I will hold this kingdom together the same way I built it—with my own strength. I can trust no one else—not even the Lord."

Scriptures influencing this chapter:

· 1 Samuel 13:6-14 – Samuel warns Saul about disobedience.
· 1 Samuel 15:13-28 – The Lord's rejection of Saul and call of another to replace him.

CHAPTER

SIX

IN THE HOUSE OF JESSE

*"The Lord looks down from heaven on all
mankind to see if there are any who
understand, any who seek God."*
—Psalm 14:2

As Samuel rounded the bend in the trail, the home of Jesse came into view. The courtyard buzzed with activity, a hum of expectation in the air. Many of the Elders were already present, huddled in animated groups, their whispers rising like the wind before a storm. On the doorstep stood a man in his finest attire, though the hurried manner of his dress suggested the urgency of the moment. Servants scurried back and forth, balancing loaves of bread, folded cloth, and other provisions, preparing for an occasion none yet understood.

As Samuel approached, the man at the door clapped his hands three times. Instantly, the commotion ceased, and all eyes turned toward the prophet. Jesse stepped forward, his wife Nitzevet at his side, their faces a mixture of awe and uncertainty.

"Welcome to our home. My name is Jesse. We are most honored by your visit. You have traveled far; will you please come and have a seat?"

Samuel bowed slightly, "Thank you, Jesse of Bethlehem. Please excuse my unannounced arrival. I know my coming has likely caused some disturbance in your household. I am not accustomed to such visits."

Nitzevet waved a hand. "It is no disturbance at all to receive a prophet of the Lord. It is a great honor. You say you are not accustomed to these types of visits; if you don't mind me asking, what kind of visit is this?"

Samuel's laugh was warm, though it did little to ease the tension in Nitzevet's voice.

"Fear not. I come to bless and to make sacrifice. But first, let us sit and talk for a while. My feet are weary from the journey, and my throat could use a drink."

Jesse led Samuel into his home and offered him the finest seat. A servant appeared almost immediately, bearing a vessel of wine that glinted ruby-red in the light. They sat in silence for a time, all of them lost in thought. Through the thin walls, Samuel could hear the crowd's murmurs of speculation, each theory more fantastic than the last.

Finally, Samuel broke the silence.

"Jesse, let me dispel the mystery of my visit. I have come by way of commandment from the Lord. He has sent me to Bethlehem to anoint a new king over Israel."

Jesse froze as the words crashed over him like a wave.

"What about King Saul? Has something happened to him? Has he been killed in battle?" Jesse asked with concern.

Samuel's gaze grew distant for a moment. "Yes, something has happened to Saul. He still lives and still sits on the throne, but something else—something far greater—has been lost." His voice trailed off, laden with sorrow, and for an instant, Jesse thought he glimpsed a tear glistening in the corner of the prophet's eye.

None of them spoke; the silence between them stretching with uncertainty and anticipation.

At last, Samuel's voice returned, "Jesse, I have come to anoint a new king. I do not yet know who it will be, but I do know this: he resides in this house. The Lord has revealed to me that the next king of Israel will be one of your sons. That is why I have come so urgently."

Jesse's mind reeled. A king? In his house? The thought was absurd, almost impossible. They were farmers and merchants, unremarkable in every way. His sons had strength and spirit, yes, but they were as far from royal as the animals they tended.

Samuel read Jesse's disbelief plainly. "I know this

comes as a shock to you, and I must admit, it is a shock to me as well. But I have learned not to question the Lord; when He commands, I obey. And He has commanded me to come here and anoint the next king of Israel. Please, gather your sons. It is time to make sacrifice and see how the Lord's plan unfolds."

SCRIPTURES INFLUENCING THIS CHAPTER:

· 1 Samuel 16:5 – Samuel consecrates Jesse's home

CHAPTER

SEVEN

THE CALLING

"You stoop down to make me great."
—Psalm 18:35

The courtyard was alive with the buzz of anticipation. The town Elders, along with the rest who had gathered, stood in a semicircle, their robes shifting softly in the breeze, their faces turned toward the house of Jesse. Overhead, the sun hung high, its golden light pooling in the dust like a divine spotlight on the unfolding events.

Jesse's sons stood in a line before the house, shoulder to shoulder, their expressions showing both pride and apprehension. They had not had time to change from their work clothes, and beads of sweat glistened on their brows. To the gathered crowd, they were a picture of rugged strength, a family ready to meet whatever awaited them.

Nobody felt the weight of the moment more than Samuel. As his eyes lingered on the faces before him, a deeper worry weighed upon his soul. He recalled with painful clarity how his anointing of Saul, once a beacon of hope for Israel, had led to a king marred by pride and disobedience. A gnawing doubt had begun to take root in the prophet's heart: What if it was his fault the kingdom was in jeopardy? What if Saul had failed as a king because Samuel had failed as his mentor? Was the Lord's rejection of the king also a rebuke of His prophet? Was the Lord now giving Samuel a chance to redeem himself with a new king?

Such questions would have to wait, the time had come to call the next king. Samuel stepped forward, the expression on his face more calm than the turmoil in his mind. He scanned the faces of Jesse's sons before closing his eyes in prayer, humbly seeking the Lord's guidance. When he opened them, his gaze landed first on Eliab, the eldest.

Eliab was tall and broad-shouldered, his stance exuding quiet confidence. Samuel studied him, his heart quickening. "Surely this is the Lord's anointed, he already bears the confidence of a king," he thought. But as he took a step closer, the quiet voice of the Lord spoke within him:

"Do not look at his appearance, Samuel, for I have not chosen him. The Lord does not see as man sees. Man looks at the outward appearance, but the Lord looks at the heart."

Samuel did not let the surprise he felt inside show on his face as he moved on to the next son. Shammah stood tall, his rough hands evidence of long hours of toil, his expression determined. This time there was no stirring in Samuel's spirit, no confirming feeling or voice at all. "Sometimes silence is also an answer," he thought to himself.

One by one, each of Jesse's sons passed before the prophet, and each time, the answer was the same. The Lord's silence lingered, leaving increasing uncertainty in its wake. Samuel's concern was growing with every passing moment.

By the time he reached the youngest son in line, Samuel's heart was near panic. This boy was barely more than a child, his frame smaller than his brothers, his face not yet hardened by the trials of manhood. Samuel hesitated. Could this really be the one?

Samuel stood there, waiting, but he again felt absolutely nothing. Where had he gone wrong? What did he miss? He turned to the side, a perplexed look on his face. Something wasn't right. He was told he would find the next king among the sons of Jesse. Yet here they were, and none had been chosen. The panic in his heart started to spread through his body. Had he lost the Lord's favor just as Saul had? Had the Lord rejected him as a prophet?

"Are these...all of your sons?" Samuel asked in confusion, turning to Jesse.

Jesse paused, a flicker of unease crossing his face.

"Actually, no," he said with reluctance. "Our youngest son, David, is out tending the flocks. I did not think to call for him because he would not be the one you are looking for."

Samuel felt a small flicker of hope spring up within him. "I need to see him. We will wait while a servant goes to fetch him."

The servants scattered as the sounds of hushed whispers and rustling bodies came from the crowd. People were growing impatient with this spectacle. Were they really going to wait for David? It seemed like a waste of time. He was too small to lead a group in prayer let alone the whole nation in war.

After what seemed like hours, a small figure appeared at the edge of the courtyard. His hair was windswept, his cheeks flushed from running. His clothes, still dusted from the fields, clung to him awkwardly. Nitzevet ran to him, trying to help David look presentable.

"Mother, what has happened? The servants told me to come immediately because Samuel the Prophet had come to our home. Is it true?"

He scanned the scene behind his mother. A large crowd had gathered. His brothers were there, standing in a straight line in front of the house from oldest to youngest. He looked at each of them, standing solemnly. When his eyes reached the end of the line, he saw another familiar face.

David gasped as his gaze settled on the old traveler

from the road, now standing in his family's courtyard. Confusion flickered in his eyes—why was the traveler here? Was he too seeking the prophet? Then, in a heartbeat, the realization struck him. The man he had spoken to earlier wasn't just an ordinary traveler, he was Samuel the Prophet.

ACROSS THE COURTYARD, Samuel froze. There, in front of him, was the shepherd boy he met outside of town. He was small and dirty yet, upon seeing him, Samuel instantly felt a wave of emotion, as if a fire had been lit inside him.

So, it was true—he had felt something earlier that day. During their conversation, he'd sensed an undeniable pull toward the boy, as though an invisible thread connected them. In that moment, he had dismissed the feeling, brushing it aside. But now, it surged back with a force that could not be ignored.

"It cannot be him," thought Samuel. "How could this small and unassuming boy lead Israel to triumph? Surely the Lord requires someone older, stronger, and more commanding."

As Samuel wrestled with his thoughts, the voice returned to his mind. It was not loud or forceful but gentle and assuring.

"Samuel, do not judge him on that which is not important to me. You see a small shepherd boy, but I have looked in his heart and found him to be worthy to be the next king of my people. He will do many great works in my name. Do not forget that you were also called when you were just a young boy."

Samuel realized he had been holding his breath and exhaled slowly, trying to release the whirlwind he was feeling inside. As David drew closer, a warmth spread through the prophet's chest, and the unmistakable voice of the Lord spoke once more:

"This is the one I have called."

Samuel stepped forward as his doubts began to dissolve. The world around him seemed to fall away until it was just he and the boy.

"We meet again, young shepherd," Samuel said, a knowing smile touching his lips. "Though when we last spoke, neither of us fully understood the significance of that meeting."

David stepped closer; his brow furrowed in thought. "This morning, on the road, you spoke of paths yet to be revealed. I didn't think this was what you meant."

Samuel nodded, his eyes steady on the young shepherd. "Nor did I. The Lord works in ways we cannot always comprehend at the time, David. It appears that our brief encounter was no accident. He was preparing us both for this moment."

"What exactly is this moment, Samuel?" David asked with growing concern.

Samuel's voice remained steady. "The Lord has sent me to call a new king of His people."

David scanned the courtyard, his gaze finally resting on his brothers. "Who is it?"

Samuel answered without words, allowing his expression to convey the message. David waited for a response from the prophet, but the answer came to him like a shock. A sensation ran through his body, causing his heart to race uncontrollably. "Me?"

Samuel only nodded.

A flurry of questions exploded in David's mind as he tried to find words to express them. In the end, he only managed to look at Samuel and mumble, "Why would the Lord choose someone like me?"

The prophet placed a calm and understanding hand on David's shoulder. "Because He sees in you what others cannot. Perhaps it is your heart, your faith, or your willingness to learn. Remember this, David: The Lord does not always call those who are most qualified; He qualifies those whom He calls—and He has called you."

David opened his mouth to speak, but no words came. He did not share the fire of conviction that burned in Samuel's eyes, confirming that this was the Lord's will. Instead, an icy chill of doubt crept through him, leaving his body trembling with fear and uncertainty.

Samuel broke the silence. "Let us make this known to all. There will be time for us to speak later."

With that, Samuel raised his voice so all could hear, though his eyes remained fixed on the shepherd.

"David, son of Jesse," he said, his voice loud yet full of reverence. "The Lord has chosen you to lead His people.

One day, you will be king over all Israel. May you prepare your heart, for the path ahead will demand all that you are and all that you will become."

Turning to the crowd, Samuel proclaimed in a loud voice, "Today we give thanks to the Lord, for His wisdom surpasses our own. Let us offer a sacrifice in His honor."

Jesse and his sons looked on, their faces a canvas of conflicting emotions—pride, confusion, envy. David's mother rushed to his side, tears in her eyes. The Elders whispered excitedly among themselves as they searched for meaning in what they had just witnessed. A king had been called in their midst, yet he defied every expectation they had.

Scriptures influencing this chapter:

· 1 Samuel 16:6-10 – Jesse's oldest sons not chosen.

· 1 Samuel 16:11 – Samuel asks if there are other sons.

· 1 Samuel 16:12 – The Lord chooses David

EIGHT

STONES ON THE ROOFTOP

"Make me to know your ways, O Lord;
teach me your paths."
—Psalm 25:4

The rest of the afternoon passed like a hazy dream for David. During the sacrifice, he stared into the flames, his thoughts swirling in chaotic patterns, each one more confusing than the last. A few of the village Elders came to offer congratulations, but their voices were drowned out by the murmur of the crowd. His brothers said nothing—and their silence hurt more than their teasing ever could.

After the sacrifice, Jesse had a meal prepared for Samuel and the Elders who lingered. The household buzzed with unease. What were they to do with David now? Should he be honored, seated at the head of the table, addressed as "majesty" or "king"? No one knew how to act, and so they chose to behave as though nothing had changed. David, sensing their discomfort, withdrew to a quiet corner where he could gather his thoughts.

From the instant Samuel had spoken the words, "He has chosen you," a storm of emotions had overtaken David: shock, awe, fear, inadequacy. Could it be true? Could he, a shepherd, be destined to lead Israel? Surely, there was a mistake.

As the evening wore on, David knew he needed to speak with Samuel, but the thought made his chest tighten. This morning, Samuel had seemed like an ordinary old traveler; now he was a great prophet who carried the will of the Lord. How could he have a conversation with such a man?

He found Samuel sitting alone on the rooftop, gazing over the city, a small lantern flickering by his side. As David drew closer, he saw that the lantern's light was illuminating a collection of peculiar stones, arranged carefully in a row in front of the prophet. They did not look particularly valuable, yet each stone was unique and beautiful in its own way.

David hesitated for a moment, afraid to interrupt the prophet's thoughts, then approached timidly.

"I was wondering when you'd come," Samuel said,

without looking up. "We haven't spoken since the sacrifice. I've been reflecting on what the Lord revealed today, and I imagine you have too. Tell me, David, what weighs on your mind?"

David sat down, folding his legs beneath him. "I'm not sure how to talk to a prophet," he admitted, his voice barely above a whisper. "And I really don't know how to talk like a king."

Samuel smiled faintly. "Then let's set aside titles. For tonight, we'll speak as two men, both searching for clarity, each trying to understand the path set before us."

David studied the stones in front of Samuel. "Why does a prophet need understanding? Doesn't the Lord tell you everything you need to know?"

"He does," Samuel replied, "but not always in ways I understand. Sometimes His commands feel too great for me to carry. Sometimes I doubt my own abilities."

David frowned. "But you're the great Samuel. Everyone knows the stories. You've performed miracles, defeated armies, spoken with the Lord Himself. Why would you ever doubt?"

Samuel looked out over the flickering lights of the city below, his voice steady. "I have often pondered that very question. As my life moves on, I have come to realize that our strength lies not in being free of doubt, but in choosing to trust the Lord in spite of it. Doubt itself is not the enemy; it can, if embraced wisely, lead us to deeper faith. The true danger is in giving up on ourselves because of our doubts—allowing them to hold us back from becoming who we are meant to be. That, David, is the greatest tragedy of all."

The prophet turned to David, his expression serious. "Do you truly believe you are destined to remain a 'nobody'?

David looked away, remembering the words from their conversation that morning. "Before today, I thought I'd grow up to be a farmer or maybe a merchant. Now you tell me I'm supposed to be a king. I don't think I'm ready for that."

"You're right," Samuel said. "Tonight, you are not ready. But many times, readiness is born within the journey, not at the beginning. Too many people miss out on the important journeys of life because they wait until they feel completely ready to start. That is a mistake. Today was an invitation for you to begin your journey, just as you are, with faith that the Lord has a plan for you."

David's voice partly faltered. "Why wouldn't the Lord pick someone who was farther along that journey than I am? It doesn't make sense to choose someone like me."

Samuel paused and then sighed. "I understand your concerns. There was another before you who had doubts just as you do, and he was not ready either. But for a time, he rose to greatness."

"What happened to him?" David asked.

"He lost his way," Samuel said simply. "That is why I am here now. The Lord has called you to take his place. Will you accept the call?"

David hesitated in astonishment as he realized that Samuel was referring to the king.

"You mean I am supposed to replace King Saul? When you said I was called to be the "future king", I thought you meant much farther down the road! How could I replace the mighty Saul?"

Samuel waited patiently for a few moments as David processed this new understanding. After a long pause he simply asked again. "Will you accept the call?"

"Wait, do you mean I have a choice?" David replied, the thought not occurring to him before now.

Samuel nodded. "The Lord forces no one. He calls and then waits patiently. Some answer the call, some run from it, and others do nothing, paralyzed by indecision. But ultimately, the choice remains yours."

A silence stretched between them. Samuel let it linger, his attention drifting back to the stones laid out in front of him. Finally, David spoke. "How did you feel when you were called to be a prophet?"

Samuel's gaze softened as his mind pulled up the memory. "I was your age. I felt unworthy, frightened, alone. People laughed at me, mocked me for daring to believe I could serve the Lord. I nearly ran away. But a wise and kind old man named Eli gave me counsel that steadied my heart."

David leaned closer. "What did he tell you?"

"He didn't say much," Samuel replied, lifting one of the stones before him. "He just gave me this stone and said, 'When you feel the weight of doubt pressing down, let this remind you what the Lord sees in you and who He has called you to become. Like this stone, His promises are solid and reliable—more than all the doubts of the world.' This stone became an anchor in my moments of greatest fear and self-doubt."

David pondered the stone in the prophet's hand, its warm red color almost seemed to glow in the lantern light. His gaze moved downward. "And these other stones, do they mean something as well?" he asked, hoping for more answers to alleviate his own doubts.

"They do," Samuel answered, "but their meanings are mine alone. Each stone carries a story, a lesson etched into the fabric of my life. They are sacred to me but may be meaningless to you."

David paused in thought. "I wish I had something to guide me through what you're asking me to do."

Samuel put a reassuring hand on David's shoulder. "My stones are precious to me because they represent wisdom gained through my struggles. You have been called to walk a difficult path David, one full of obstacles and adversity, and you have many lessons to learn before you reach your destiny. Perhaps you will find stones of your own to remind you of those lessons."

David's voice wavered. "I'm not sure I can take that path. Saul is everything the people admire—a warrior, a leader, a king. I am none of those things, who would follow me?"

Samuel met his gaze with understanding. "The Lord

has chosen you not only for who you are but for who you can become. He sees a king in you, David, though you may not see it in yourself. He has opened a door for you and shown you a path to take. If you accept the Lord's call, you will be expected to improve and prepare yourself for the day when you become king, even though we don't know when that will be.

Do you remember the stories about the Lord calling our ancestors out of Egypt? They had to travel a great distance through an unknown wilderness and suffer many hardships before they were prepared and found worthy to inherit this Promised Land. In the same way, greatness awaits you if you will take the journey through your own wilderness and become what the Lord needs you to become. Nobody will force you to move forward. It must come from you."

With that, Samuel slowly rose to his feet, gathering his stones carefully into a pouch. "It is getting late, and I am weary from the events of the day. Spend some time alone to consider all we've talked about and then listen for the voice of the Lord. He has called you and He will guide you. I must leave for Ramah tomorrow at midday. I will wait for your answer until then."

Without another word, Samuel descended from the rooftop, leaving David alone with his thoughts beneath the vast, star-filled sky.

~

SCRIPTURES INFLUENCING THIS CHAPTER:

- 1 Samuel 9:26 – Samuel teaches on rooftops.
- 1 Samuel 3 – Samuel also called at a young age.
- Joshua 3 – Israelites pass into the Promised Land.

NINE

THE CHOICE

*"The Lord upholds all who fall
and lifts up all who are bowed down."*
—Psalm 145:14

The next morning, David sat beneath the shade of a familiar tree, his staff resting beside him, while his flock grazed peacefully on the dew-laden grass. The night's restless thoughts still clung to him like cobwebs, refusing to clear. He had come here early, long before the sun rose, hoping the solitude of the hills might offer clarity; yet the same questions plagued him, circling endlessly in his mind.

"What am I supposed to do?" he murmured to the sheep grazing nearby. "I can't be a shepherd forever, but I know I could never be a king. If I accept Samuel's call, I'll have to leave behind everything I know to enter a world full of people just like my brothers—people who will only mock me. Who would ever follow someone like me? I'm not respected in my own family, let alone worthy of leading a nation. I'm nobody. Samuel will understand if I don't go. He must see that this is a mistake. I can't be the one."

The sheep, as always, offered no answers. They simply grazed, their quiet presence a small comfort.

"Yes, Samuel was mistaken," he declared. "The Lord will call someone else. Someone stronger, someone wiser."

But deep down, unable to be buried by his doubts, David felt the truth. Samuel's words had carried a power that could not be denied. The Lord had chosen him. He did not understand why, but the choice was made, and he could feel it in his heart. So why was he so reluctant to accept it? He always wanted to be more than a shepherd, but now that the opportunity he longed for had arrived, he found himself afraid to take it. Why was he letting his doubts be more convincing than his destiny?

The morning air grew still and the sheep began shifting nervously, sensing something. David was so lost in thought that he never saw the movement in the grass, creeping slowly towards them. Sudden and frantic bleating snapped him to attention. He looked up to see his flock running towards him in a panicked manner. One of the sheep had spotted the danger and signaled the others to scatter. David took a step forward but froze as a lion sprang from its crouched position and began its pursuit.

David stood motionless; his feet rooted to the ground as if the weight of his fear had anchored him in place. He knew what he should do, but the courage to act eluded him once again. He knew this lion. This was not the first time it had attacked his flock. Each time, a few precious sheep were dragged away, and each time, David could do nothing but watch helplessly, paralyzed by terror. This time, it seemed, would be no different.

The world slowed to a crawl as he watched the scene unfold in front of him. The only sound he could hear was the rapid thumping of his heart. The lion was closing fast on one of the young lambs and would soon pounce.

Suddenly, a voice interrupted David's panicked thoughts.

"You must save them", it said.

David heard the voice clearly, but its origin was a mystery, as if spoken by an invisible figure at his side.

Focusing intently on the scene before him, David tried to ignore the voice.

"You must act. Only you can save them." The voice rang again, perfectly clear in his ear.

"I can't." David thought. "That lion is so strong. I cannot stop it. It will kill me."

The voice came back a third time, louder and more

penetrating than ever. "If you do not try, your sheep will die. You are their protector; you are the only one that can stop the enemy from destroying them."

Tears formed in David's eyes as his body began to shake. He held his breath for a moment and then slumped his shoulders in surrender. "I can't. I am not enough."

Although David held everything he needed to intervene, he could do nothing more than watch as the lion finally pounced upon the lamb, taking it down in one swift motion. The lamb's cries felt like daggers piercing David's heart.

Fortunately, the lion did not pursue the others. Content with its kill, it lifted the lifeless lamb in its mouth and carried it away. David watched, trembling in place, the tears now running down his cheeks.

"I let this happen." he said to himself. "By doing nothing I let that lamb die. But what could I have done? If I had used my sling and missed, it would have still taken the lamb. If I had rushed in, the lion would have killed us both."

As David sat in silence, the voice returned, although a little softer.

"How many will you allow to die before you decide to take action?"

David spoke out loud even though he knew there was nobody there. "I lose a few each year but I still have the rest."

"How long will it be until you have none left?" the voice replied.

The question struck David deeply, and he found meaning far beyond the immediate circumstances. In a moment of clarity, he realized that this was about more than his flock. Ever since he was very young, he had dreams of becoming something more than a shepherd or a farmer, but they had remained just that—dreams. Doubt whispered that he wasn't good enough and fear argued that the journey was too long and the effort too great. Slowly, the belief in his dreams had withered, like fruit left untended on the vine. How many dreams had he buried already? How long until there were no more dreams left to lose?

David didn't need to hear a voice this time, the chastising words formed in his mind on their own. They were your responsibility. What you do, or decide not to do, makes a difference. When the opportunities arise, you must act. If you do not, you will suffer a million defeats in your lifetime.

"I need to act," David said aloud, his voice trembling but resolute as the frightened sheep gathered around him. "I am not meant to remain a shepherd. I love you, my little flock, but today I see that my love alone is not enough. I thought I was your protector, but when the lion came, I let fear paralyze me again. If I am to be more than this, I must learn to face what I fear and to act even when doubt consumes me. If I wish to fulfill any purpose, I must stop running away. Today, I will take the first step. Today, I am going to seize the opportunity the Lord has placed before me and take control of my life."

SCRIPTURES INFLUENCING THIS CHAPTER:

· 1 Samuel 17:34 – David talks about encounters with predators while watching his flock.

TEN

THE ANOINTING

"You anoint my head with oil;
my cup overflows."
—Psalm 23:5

J esse's servants were busy loading Samuel's pack onto a mule when David came sprinting around the corner, his breaths ragged and labored. He pushed his way through the groups of Elders and towns-people that had gathered to see the prophet's departure.

"Where is the prophet? Has Samuel left yet?" David managed between gasps.

"He's inside, bidding farewell to your father," one of the servants replied without pausing in their work.

David let out a shaky breath of relief, bending over to

place his hands on his knees. The morning's events had drained him; the emotional toll of the lion attack still clung to him. Yet, he managed to secure his flock and race up the hill in time to meet the prophet.

As if summoned by David's thoughts, Samuel emerged from the house, Jesse close behind. The prophet's eyes fell on David, and a smile softened his weathered face. Jesse lingered near the doorway, his expression unreadable, as Samuel approached the young shepherd.

"Walk with me," Samuel said, his tone firm but inviting.

David hesitated for a few breaths, his legs still trembling from the sprint. He forced himself upright and nodded. Together, they began walking toward the edge of the courtyard, away from prying eyes.

Samuel broke the silence first. "You left early this morning. I was unsure whether I would see you again."

"I needed time to think," David admitted, his voice quiet.

"And what did your thinking do for you?" Samuel asked.

David considered the question. "Actually, thinking did nothing for me today. A lion came for my sheep and all I could do was watch helplessly. I was frozen by fear. I lost another one today because, like always, I did nothing to stop it. I'm done thinking and I'm done being scared. I want to be a man of action."

Samuel turned his full attention to David. "And this is why you've returned?"

"It is. I am still afraid that I will fail as a king, but the thought of being someone who always stands idle, watching life pass by without action, terrifies me even more. I learned that lesson today when the lion took my sheep."

Samuel nodded solemnly. "That is good. The decision to act in the face of fear will serve you well in the days to come. Becoming a king will not be easy, David. It is a journey fraught with challenges. There will be those who guide you and others who try to tear you down. There will be times when you feel your growth and times when failure seems inevitable. But if you choose to take action, you will find a strength you did not know you had. The Lord chose you because He knows you better than you know yourself, and He sees greatness in you."

The prophet's words settled in David's heart like a gentle rain soaking parched earth. David closed his eyes as he felt a calming warmth spread through his body. Finally, he spoke. "I heard a voice today when the lion attacked. It was as if someone was standing beside me, but nobody was there."

Samuel's expression shifted, his eyes narrowing with interest. "What did the voice say?"

"It told me to go and save my sheep," David said. "It wasn't loud, but it cut straight through to my heart, like the person speaking could see into my soul. It knew I was scared, but it didn't scold me. It just...understood, and then urged me to do something."

Samuel remained quiet, his gaze distant, as if searching for a memory. Finally, he said, "I know that voice well. I first heard it when I was your age. It will come to you again when you need it most. Listen to it, David, and always do as it says. It is the call of the Master."

David's grip tightened around the staff he carried. "That voice, the...uh...Master, made me realize something. My sheep have been taken by predators over the years, just as my dreams have been taken by fear. I can't let that happen anymore because eventually I will have none left. I don't want to live a life wondering what might have been."

Samuel stopped walking and turned to face him fully. His voice carried a strength that silenced the breeze. "You've made your decision then?"

David straightened his posture. "I have. I will accept the calling to become the king. Although I am scared and I know it will not be easy, I know it is right, and I know it is what the Lord wants for me. Today is the day I choose to act in the face of my fear."

Samuel smiled then took David by the arm. With measured steps, he directed David back to the center of the courtyard, where Jesse, Nitzevet, and the elders waited. The murmurs ceased as Samuel motioned for silence. Samuel retrieved the hollow ram's horn from his pack and raised it above David's head.

"David, son of Jesse," Samuel proclaimed, "with this oil, I anoint you as the future king of Israel. May the Lord guide your steps, shape your heart, and prepare you for the day when you will take the throne. Use this time to grow into the man He has called you to be."

Oil poured out of the horn, shimmering in the morning light as it flowed over David's hair and shoulders. Jesse watched with pride, though his eyes held traces of concern. The Elders exchanged glances, their faces a mixture of awe and uncertainty. David tried to stay calm and reverent, even though on the inside he felt the fire of nervous excitement that always comes from taking one step closer to your destiny.

As Samuel stepped back, his task complete, he placed a hand on David's shoulder. "Your journey begins now, but your path will not be straight. Do not rush it. The Lord will prepare you in His time and in His way. It will not always make sense to you. Be patient and be ready."

Reaching into the folds of his robe, Samuel withdrew a smooth, red stone, its surface glinting faintly in the sunlight. David recognized it as the stone Samuel had shown him the night before. Samuel placed it in David's hand and closed his fingers gently around it.

"This stone represents vision," Samuel said, his voice steady and deliberate. "It was given to me by a great man when I was young and  now, I want to pass it to you. It is a reminder of what the Lord sees in you, even when you cannot see it yourself. When the path is unclear and doubt clouds your mind, let this stone remind you of the great man you are called to become. Do not lose sight of who you are meant to be, David, and that will help you know which paths to take and which to avoid."

David looked down at the stone, turning it over in his hand. "Thank you, Samuel," he said quietly. "I will keep it with me always, to remember this day and the calling I must live up to."

Samuel smiled, his gaze filled with both hope and pride. "Then go, young shepherd, and begin preparing. The Lord has chosen you, and He will walk with you every step of the way. Listen for His voice."

David nodded, the cool sensation of the oil still lingering. "I promise I will prepare. I will work every day to be ready."

"Good. Then there is one last piece of advice I can give you, David. It is good to take action, but your actions must lead you to become a better man. You are destined to become a king, but reaching your destination is not as important as the person you become through the journey. Becoming a king does not make you a great man, but becoming a great man will make you a king worth following."

The prophet looked to the distant horizon. "I must go now. Be ready, David. Listen to the voice of the Lord and He will guide your paths. We will meet again."

With that, Samuel turned and led his mule down the

path towards the center of the town. David, and all those assembled, watched him go, leaving behind more questions than answers.

SCRIPTURES INFLUENCING THIS CHAPTER:

· 1 Samuel 16:13 – Samuel anoints David

ELEVEN

FIRST STEPS

"You make known to me the path of life;
in your presence there is fullness of joy."
—Psalm 16:11

David turned toward the hills, the familiar landscape now bearing new significance. As he walked, each blade of grass and every stone underfoot seemed to hum with unseen potential. He clenched his staff, the wood smooth beneath his fingers, and exhaled deeply. For the first time since Samuel had left that morning, he was alone with his thoughts.

As he walked, he reflected, "My life will never be the same. I am no longer just a shepherd but a future king. At some point I will leave these sheep behind to lead an entire nation."

The thought brought with it a mixture of excitement, nervousness, and sadness. A path had been opened to him, leading to a future greater than he could have ever imagined, yet at this moment he realized just how much he would miss his flock and this hillside. This was where he felt most at home, away from the mockery of his brothers and constant reminders of his place in the family. He could be himself on this hillside and speak openly about both his worries and his dreams. The thought of leaving it behind to journey into the unknown brought an ache to his heart.

David pulled Samuel's red stone from his pouch. He turned it over in his hand as he walked, hoping to find some comfort in what it represented. As the late afternoon sun warmed his face, his swirling thoughts began to take form, bringing new clarity and insight.

"Maybe vision means not just believing in the journey ahead but appreciating the road already traveled, no matter what it was. This is not the end of one story and the beginning of another," he realized. "It is just the turning of a page, a transition from one chapter to the next in the unfolding story of my life. The boy I was yesterday doesn't get left behind—he will walk beside me, shaping the path toward the man I hope to become. My past is not a shadow to escape, but the foundation I will need for the road ahead. A part of me will always be a shepherd boy, and maybe that will somehow help me become a great king."

David smiled, pleased to have found meaning in the life he had previously wanted to escape. Until the Lord's path for him revealed itself, the sheep would still need tending and the hills still held their perils, but now every act would carry more significance and deeper purpose.

"I will never call myself 'just a shepherd' again" he added resolutely.

The world seemed to hold its breath as David moved toward the tree where his flock often rested. Each step forward marked a silent promise—to his God, to his people, and to himself—that he would grow into the man worthy of the crown waiting in the distance.

TWELVE

A TORMENTED KING

*"Why are you cast down, O my soul,
and why are you in turmoil within me?"*
—Psalm 42:5

The King of Israel sat on his throne of roughly hewn stone. Its jagged edges and uneven surface betrayed a hurried craftsmanship—a symbol, perhaps, of the rushed expectations placed upon the king himself. Yet Saul paid it no mind; his thoughts were far heavier than the discomfort of the throne.

For weeks on end, his days had been taxing and his nights restless. The weight of kingship bore down on him like a millstone, and he did not have the humility to understand why it felt more burdensome than ever. Over time, the memory of Samuel's warning had faded, and

Saul had once again convinced himself that he was the Lord's chosen ruler of Israel.

The king had grown accustomed to the prophet's disapproval, but lately it seemed as though nothing Saul did could satisfy the people either. Despite victory after victory against their enemies, whispers of discontent echoed through the courts and throughout his kingdom. The people who once rallied behind him, now criticized his rule, and plotted his demise. Kingship, once an honor, had become an unrelenting trial.

Sitting alone in the throne room, Saul's mind wandered back to simpler days—days before the throne —when his life was full of promise. He was tall, young, and striking—the son of a wealthy merchant, admired and respected. His future had seemed bright and assured, moving along exactly as planned...until he met Samuel.

It was a peculiar chain of events that led to his anointing. Sent by his father to find a herd of lost donkeys, Saul had wandered from village to village without success. At a well where maidens drew water, he heard of a prophet staying in a nearby village—a man who might offer divine guidance in his search.

Saul hurried to the village, where he encountered an old man in priestly robes. "Do you know where I can find the prophet?" Saul asked.

"Prophets are not easy to find," the man replied. "What do you seek?"

Saul responded timidly, "I need help finding my

father's lost donkeys. They have been missing for days and we do not know where to search."

Saying it out loud made Saul feel foolish. Why would a prophet of God waste his time giving insight about lost animals?

The old man's reply was unexpected: "Forget the donkeys; they have already been found. It is you, Saul, that all of Israel seeks. My name is Samuel, and I am a prophet of the Lord. The people cry for a king, and the Lord has chosen you."

Saul had chuckled at the seemingly absurd words of the prophet, but the piercing intensity in Samuel's gaze quickly silenced him, leaving no doubt that it was a moment of profound seriousness.

From that point onward, Saul's life became a whirlwind of events. He spent hours speaking with Samuel, who anointed him as the king of all Israel that very day. Just a few weeks later, he stood before the people as the chosen one to reunite Israel. The army rallied behind him, and under his leadership, victories against Israel's enemies came swiftly. All of Israel united under his rule, heralding him as their greatest leader since Joshua.

And yet, despite the accolades and triumphs, Saul now felt an unshakable misery deep within him.

"Curse the day I met Samuel," he said out loud. "My life was fine until he forced me onto this throne. It has become nothing but an endless list of rigid rules and unyielding expectations, each one demanding more than what I have to give."

Footsteps approached and a servant cautiously entered the room.

"Did you call my king? I thought I heard you speaking."

Saul shook himself free from his brooding. "All is not well with me, Hophas. I am constantly tormented. I cannot sleep, I have no desire to eat, and I feel empty inside. I feel as though my enemies are all around me even when I am out of danger. Something is not well with me."

"Would you like me to seek your physician?" the servant asked.

"I don't need a doctor. My body is well, it is my soul that is tormented." the king said, shifting on the throne.

"Perhaps I could call for Samuel then?" Hophas asked.

"Bah, Samuel." the king spat. "Some prophet he is. Constantly reminding me of how much of a failure I am. He's never happy no matter how much I succeed. I've conquered our enemies, united our people, and ruled with wisdom, yet *he* claims the Lord is angry with me. I definitely don't need Samuel right now."

Hophas nodded his head. "I understand, my king. Might I suggest some music. It has helped me to feel calm in times of distress."

Saul was grateful for the alternative to Samuel. "Thank you Hophas, that sounds wonderful. Call the court musicians."

Hophas paused, his voice betraying the nervousness he felt. "Begging your pardon, my king. Might I make another suggestion?"

"Yes, what is it?" Saul replied impatiently.

Hophas began timidly, "It may be wise to avoid letting people know how you are feeling. An entire group of court musicians may spread rumors. A few months ago, I was traveling near the town of Bethlehem. As I moved down the road, I heard beautiful music coming from the hillside. I followed the sound and found a shepherd boy playing the harp. The music was so peaceful and calming that I stopped my travels to listen for a while. The sound was like nothing I had ever heard. Might I send for this boy and bring him here to play for you when you are feeling unsettled?"

Saul took a breath before answering in resignation. "I trust your judgment, Hophas. But please hurry, I feel as though the weight of this crown will crush me."

Scriptures influencing this chapter:

· 1 Samuel 16:14-15 – King Saul is tormented.

· 1 Samuel 9-15 – Saul's history with Samuel

· 1 Samuel 16:16-18 – Saul's advisors recommend music to calm him. One servant remembers David.

THIRTEEN

THE SUMMONS

*"I will instruct you and teach you in the
way you should go; I will counsel you
with my loving eye on you."*
—Psalm 32:8

The sun hung high over the hills of Bethlehem, bathing them in golden light. David sat beneath the shade of a gnarled olive tree; an old harp cradled in his arms. His fingers absentmindedly plucked at the strings, weaving a soft melody that mingled with the gentle bleating of his sheep, who were scattered across the hillside grazing peacefully.

This had become David's daily routine. There had been a flurry of excitement and preparation in the weeks following the anointing by Samuel, but as day led to day and the weeks rolled on, David began to fall back into his old, familiar life. Without a clear timeline of when he needed to be ready, his resolve to prepare every day began to falter. Frustrated by the lack of direction, he convinced himself that waiting for a sign from the Lord was all he could do, though deep down, the stillness left him restless and impatient for something more.

A shadow fell over David, breaking his moment of reflection. He looked up to see a familiar man standing before him, dressed in the fine garments of the king's court. David stood, clutching his harp as familiarity and curiosity mingled in his expression.

The man inclined his head, his expression one of urgency. "Young shepherd, my name is Hophas, you may remember that we've met before. I am a servant of King Saul, and I come with a summons directly from the king himself. He requests your presence at the palace in Gibeah."

David's brow furrowed. "The king summons *me*? Why? How would he even know me?"

Hophas smiled faintly, as if recalling their first encounter. "The king has heard of your skill with the harp —I told him of the day I heard you play here in the hills. Lately he has been troubled in spirit and believes your music may bring him peace."

David's heart quickened. The king? Saul himself? A rush of thoughts filled his mind—excitement, purpose, fear, and doubt all battling for space.

"I am honored by the king's summons," David began

slowly as doubt crept up inside him, "but I have responsibilities here to my flock and my family. I don't know if I could just leave."

David didn't know why he said it, and it instantly sounded ridiculous as the words left his mouth. Who turns down a summons from the king in order to watch sheep?

Hophas' expression changed. "I understand your hesitation, young shepherd, but this is a command directly from the king. To refuse would be to defy him and I can assure you, that would be unwise. Surely your family or another shepherd could tend the flock in your absence?"

David turned his gaze to the sheep, his mind caught in a conflict between doubt and possibility. Samuel had told him to have faith and watch for signs from the Lord. Now this messenger arrives summoning him to the court of Saul. This must be the opportunity he needed to take, the next step on his journey to become the king. The palace would be a place where he could learn the ways of leadership and take the first steps toward the throne he had been anointed for. Perhaps this was not simply the call of King Saul, but the call of destiny itself. Now was the time to put his fear behind him and act.

He stood and opened his mouth to speak, but something stopped him. A warm breeze had suddenly rustled in the branches of the tree, and within it, David caught the faintest whisper, a voice both strong yet tender: *"Remain with your sheep."*

David paused. Had he really heard that? He closed his

eyes and tried to listen to the wind, certain he had imagined the voice. It came again, more clearly this time: "Remain with your sheep. There are lessons still to be learned here. The time for the palace has not yet come."

David's eyes snapped open, his heart wavering. Was that the voice of the Lord again? The same voice that spoke when the lion came for his sheep, the one that Samuel said to always listen to? Or was it the wind giving voice to his own nervousness and fear?

In the moment of hesitation, David's mind took over from his heart. Certainly this summons from the king was the next step in his path to the throne, why else would a king's servant seek out a lowly shepherd? This was his opportunity to leave his fear behind and take a bold step towards who he was meant to be. Surely the voice in the wind was only the voice of his own doubting mind.

"I can't listen to my doubts anymore." he whispered to himself.

"Very well," David said, turning his attention back to Hophas. "I will go to serve the king. But I must first ensure the safety of my flock."

Hophas smiled. "The king will be pleased. Shall I wait while you make arrangements?"

David moved swiftly, gathering his sheep and leading them into the fold. He called to his brother Eliab, who was laboring nearby, and explained the situation. Eliab's expression darkened as he listened. "So this is it, huh? You're just going to run off to the king's palace and claim the throne?" he said, his voice sharp with bitterness. "And you're leaving us behind to do your work tending the sheep while you chase your so-called destiny?"

David didn't know what to say, the thought of it did sound foolish coming from his brother's mouth.

After an awkward silence, he responded, "This is what I'm supposed to do. You remember what happened when Samuel came to our village, and you heard what he anointed me to become."

Eliab laughed mockingly. "David, wake up. That old prophet's time has passed and now he just wanders the land telling stories and putting ideas in the heads of children. We already have a king, and the Lord has made him strong and victorious in battle. Do you really believe you are better than King Saul?"

David felt the pain of his brother's words. They reflected the way many had treated him ever since Samuel's visit. The general feeling in Bethlehem, especially among the Elders, was that Samuel had made a mistake and that the Lord was no longer with him. Why else would he act so strangely and anoint a shepherd boy to become the king? The thought of it was absurd.

Not knowing how to respond to Eliab's accusations, David awkwardly handed over his staff. "Just keep watch over them as you would your own," he said, his voice full of uncertainty. "I will return as soon as I am able."

The words felt hollow, for he thought that this might mark the last time he would ever see his sheep.

Eliab turned and stomped away, unsettled by the sudden attention lavished on his youngest brother. As the firstborn and heir to the family's legacy, he wasn't accustomed to standing in anyone's shadow—especially not David's. And it gnawed at him.

A short time later, David stood at the threshold of his home, a pack slung over one shoulder, his harp under his arm. Hophas waited just beyond the doorway, giving the family space for their goodbyes. Nitzevet, weary-eyed yet proud, cupped her youngest son's face with both hands.

"It is so soon, but I know the Lord has set a path for you, my son," she affirmed, her voice steady despite the emotion in her eyes. "Walk it with humility, and never forget who you are, no matter what riches or power you may find in the palace." She lovingly brushed his cheek with her thumb.

David swallowed the lump in his throat, nodding as he pressed his forehead against hers for a moment.

He turned to his father who gave him a slow nod before stepping forward.

"Son," Jesse said, his voice firm. "This is no small thing you're walking into. You've been given an opportunity, but don't think for a second that opportunity alone makes a man great. A man is measured by what he does with what he's given." He placed a firm hand on David's shoulder and looked him directly in the eye before adding, "So don't waste it; do you hear me? What you do reflects on our entire family now."

David let out a small, breathy laugh, a release of tension he hadn't realized he was holding. "I hear you father. I won't let you down."

Jesse nodded, satisfied, then stepped back.

Nitzevet wiped at her eyes, smiling as she lifted her hands. "Go with God, my son."

David turned to Hophas, exhaling slowly as he took his first step away from home. As they left the city, he glanced back at the hills he had tended for so long. Something inside him felt uneasy. The voice of the Lord still lingered in a corner of his heart, telling him it was wrong to leave, but his mind spoke more loudly, convincing him that this was the step he needed to take. Why else would such a seemingly miraculous opportunity present itself?

"This couldn't be luck or coincidence," he reasoned. "This has to be the Lord showing me the next step in my journey."

SCRIPTURES INFLUENCING THIS CHAPTER:

· 1 Samuel 16:19 – David summoned to play for Saul.

CHAPTER

FOURTEEN

ON THE ROAD TO GIBEAH

*"Even though I walk through the valley
of the shadow of death, I will fear no evil,
for you are with me."*
—Psalm 23:4

The afternoon sun cast long shadows over the dusty road as David and Hophas made their way toward Gibeah. The journey stretched ahead, winding through valleys and over rolling hills, the familiar terrain of Bethlehem slowly fading behind them. David adjusted the strap of his pack, his mind buzzing with questions he hadn't yet found the courage to ask.

For a time, they walked in silence, the only sounds being their footsteps crunching against the dirt and the occasional chirp of a bird. But David's thoughts refused to settle. He turned to Hophas, studying the man's measured stride and steady expression. Finally, he spoke.

"What is it like?" he asked. "The palace? The king?"

Hophas exhaled through his nose, as if considering how much he should say. "Gibeah is the center of power and the heart of the kingdom...but it is not what it once was," he admitted. "When Saul was first anointed, there was excitement and strength in his rule, a fire that united the people because the Lord was with us in every battle. But now?" He shook his head. "There is a shadow over the palace. I'm not exactly sure what happened, but the king grows restless, troubled by unseen burdens. He trusts fewer men each day, and those he does trust whisper behind his back more than anything."

David frowned. "Why? What's changed?"

Hophas hesitated before answering. "A king carries the weight of the people, David, but he need not carry it alone. The Lord has promised to lift the burdens of His people if they trust in Him. But power drives men to pride and eventually isolation. It is a heavy thing, and fear is its constant companion. I have been around power long enough to see what happens when a man becomes too proud of his own accomplishments and fears losing what he holds. As they try to control the world around them, they become paranoid, quick-tempered, and sometimes cruel."

David absorbed the words, his hands fidgeting with the strap of his pack. "And you think the king is afraid?"

"I know he is," Hophas said plainly. "I can see it in the way he acts. He is a man at war with himself." He cast a sidelong glance at David. "You are young, but you are not blind. You will see it soon enough."

David let the words settle, uncertainty creeping into his thoughts. "Then what am I supposed to do there? I don't think a boy with a harp will be able to solve the king's problems."

Hophas chuckled, "My hope is that you will help the king with the burden of ruling the nation. I think that your music might lighten the heaviness that rests upon him from time to time. Perhaps, if he can get a few moments of calm, his mind will clear, and he can return to being the king we were all inspired to follow."

David mulled over the words in silence. He hadn't realized the extent of the turmoil he was headed into. Was he really supposed to save the king from despair just by playing his harp? It didn't make sense, but then again, nothing about his life made sense anymore. So, for now, he decided he would just continue to walk forward, one step at a time.

As they walked on in silence, David pondered the concerning words of Hophas. King Saul seemed like someone you did not want to disappoint or disagree with. Suddenly, David had a terrifying realization: He was on his way to serve the very king that he was meant to replace. What if King Saul found out? Or worse, what if he already knew and this summons was a way to bring David to the palace to execute him?

David began to doubt his decision to leave Bethlehem and, for the first time since leaving, gave a second thought to the voice that had told him to stay.

CHAPTER

FIFTEEN

IN THE COURT OF THE KING

"You prepare a table before me
in the presence of my enemies."
—Psalm 23:5

When they arrived at the city gates, David's breath caught. The walls of Gibeah loomed above him, bathing the road in shadows. The clang of metal rang through the air as soldiers sparred in a courtyard, their swords flashing under the sun. Merchants bustled past him, their hurried steps kicking up the scent of spices and burning torches. As Hophas led him through the busy streets and into the palace, David realized this was a world far removed from the quiet streets of Bethlehem.

They were led to the throne room by a palace servant but before he could announce their arrival, a booming and angry voice echoed throughout the chamber.

"You dare bring me this news?" roared the voice, cracking through the chamber like a whip. "Where were our watchmen? Where was the warning?"

King Saul stood in the center of the grand hall, not upon his throne but pacing in short, volatile strides. His fists clenched and unclenched at his sides, his eyes blazing beneath furrowed brows. A messenger knelt before him, head bowed low, shoulders trembling.

"My king," the messenger stammered, "we do not know how the Philistine forces crossed our borders, but they are now camped inside our lands. Several outlying villages lie in their path."

Saul's eyes narrowed to slits. "Then they had help," he growled. "No enemy marches unseen into our lands unless guided. There are traitors in our midst—Israelites, posing as loyal, while feeding our enemies information from within!"

A hush fell over the court. No one dared to speak.

Saul turned sharply to his advisors. His voice, now cold and calculated, cut through the silence. "What village lies nearest the border breach?"

The advisors exchanged nervous glances before one stepped forward. "Libnah, my king. A village set aside for the priests of the tribe of Judah."

Saul's mouth twisted in contempt. "Libnah," he repeated, spitting the name like poison. "A place 'set apart' indeed. Set apart to conspire against me, no doubt. Those so-called priests always think they are above my authority. I see it now—they have opened our gates to the Philistines because they are jealous of my strength and the victories the Lord has given me."

An elderly advisor took a cautious step forward. "My king, with respect—Libnah has long been faithful, both to the Lord and to you. They would never consort with our enemies."

"Silence!" Saul snapped, his glare sharp as a blade. "They have betrayed me. I will not let this treachery spread like rot beneath the surface of my kingdom. They must be dealt with quickly as a message to any others who would betray me."

He turned to one of his commanders, a man named Abner, his voice rising. "Where is the army of my son, Jonathan, stationed?"

Abner thought for a moment before answering, "He and his men are fortifying the city of Lachish, not far from Libnah."

"Excellent." Saul said thoughtfully. "Send word to Jonathan immediately. Tell him to take his men to Libnah, surround the village, and burn it to the ground."

Gasps rippled through the chamber.

The commander, clearly shaken, spoke with hesitation. "And... the villagers, my king? Shall I have Jonathan bring them here for questioning?"

Saul's face hardened as a sneer slowly spread across his lips. "No. Just as the Lord commanded me regarding the Amalekites, so now I command you—tell him not to spare anything. Man, woman, child, beast—let it all be burned. This is the price of betrayal!"

A stunned silence gripped the court. No one moved. No one dared to breathe. David suddenly felt like he needed to say something and began to step forward, but Hophas put a hand on his shoulder to keep him in place.

Abner hesitated, "My king, you are correct that the people of Libnah must pay for their actions, but I am not sure that Jonathan will accept this order. You know your son well, it is not in his nature to carry out such an act. Let me go and take care of this for you. I will ensure that all of Israel knows the penalty for betraying their king."

Saul thought for a moment before nodding in agreement. "You are right Abner; my son's heart is too soft to do what is necessary. Go yourself, take the right kind of men with you, and destroy everything. Everything! Let Libnah be a lesson to all my kingdom that I will not be betrayed or questioned!"

The messenger, still kneeling, had begun to weep uncontrollably. A guard stepped forward and took him firmly by the arm, escorting him away as his sobs echoed down the stone corridors.

From his place at the entrance, David stood frozen, watching. This was the king? The man anointed by the Lord? David had imagined this moment many times during his journey. He had expected to meet a ruler robed in righteous strength and wisdom. Instead, what he saw was exactly as Hophas had described—the king was a man at war with himself and seemingly with everyone around him, consumed by the desire for power and haunted by the shadow of paranoia.

The king sat back on his throne, his eyes angrily fixed on the floor, as the uneasy silence continued to fill the room. Eventually, when the tension began to settle, Hophas announced his return.

"My king, I have brought the musician I spoke of. His name is David of the tribe of Judah."

Saul looked up, his eyes landing on the shepherd boy who stood timidly before him, harp in hand. He was slight of frame, barely more than a child, but there was something about him that caught the king's attention, though he could not say what. Although the boy was small and insignificant, he had a presence about him that seemed to calm the entire room.

A troubling thought suddenly stirred in the back of Saul's mind—the unsettling memory of the old prophet's warning that he would one day be replaced by another. He shook it off. That's ridiculous. The boy was here to play music, nothing more.

Saul broke the silence: "You're the one with the harp," he said in a voice that was low but still sharp.

David bowed quickly. "Yes, my king."

"My servant Hophas says that you play magnificently. At times, the burdens of kingship weigh heavily on me. Music seems to help me relax and think more clearly. You will be ready to play your harp for me whenever I call for you. In return, you will live here in the palace and may partake of the many luxuries available."

David spoke, his voice barely loud enough to be heard by the king.

"It would be a great honor for me to serve the king in any way that I can. May I?" he added, lifting his harp.

Saul nodded and took a seat on the throne. "Play. And play well. I don't need another disappointment."

As David's fingers danced over the strings, a hush fell over the room. The advisors all turned to listen more closely. The notes rose, weaving through the air like a whispered psalm, spreading to every corner of the room. The tension in Saul's shoulders loosened, and for the first time in days, the storm in his mind stilled—if only for a moment. His throne did not feel so heavy, his burdens not so suffocating. Certainly, there was something special about this boy.

Scriptures influencing this chapter:

· 1 Samuel 17:55 – Abner listed as the commander of the army.

· 1 Samuel 17:21-22 – David enters Saul's service.

SIXTEEN

WISDOM

*"I will instruct you and teach you
in the way you should go; I will counsel
you with my loving eye on you."*
—Psalm 32:8

Day after day, David was called to play for King Saul. He was summoned at all hours, day and night, whenever the king needed him. Though Saul rarely spoke to him, David could see the calming effect his music had on the king's soul, and he felt proud that he had a talent to offer such an important man.

When not playing for the king, David wandered through the palace, which was a world unto itself. He enjoyed reading from the scrolls in the palace library, conversing with wise men and advisors, or watching soldiers train for battle. If this was where he was supposed to be, he wanted to take advantage of every opportunity to learn.

He found a surprising amount of wisdom among the servants who worked in the palace. They were the easiest to talk to and always gave him good advice when he helped them with their work.

"Always be curious." an old washerwoman had told him one day as he helped her scrub the clothing in a large tub. "Every experience carries the seed of wisdom. The more curious you are about the world around you, the more seeds you will plant and therefore the more wisdom you will harvest. Don't be afraid to ask, 'Why?'; but more importantly, don't be afraid to ask, 'Why not?'"

"Every small task is an opportunity to show the type of person you are," said a young man who was cleaning the stables. "How you do anything is how you do everything. When you are faithful in the small things, the Lord blesses you with bigger things. I don't plan on working the stables forever, but if the world sees that I don't put my full effort into this task, why would I be trusted with a greater opportunity? I think the secret to getting ahead is treating the smallest tasks with just as much effort as I would the big ones."

The young man's words caused David to reflect on the time he had spent tending his sheep. Had he treated that task with the diligence it deserved before jumping to the next step in his journey? Although he loved his flock, he had never fully learned how to protect them from the predators that constantly roamed the area. The thought caused feelings of sadness and regret to stir in his heart.

David decided to spend more time among the servants and less time in the palace library. Not only for their wisdom, but because they reminded him of the people he knew back home in Bethlehem; and this brought David a measure of peace at times when he felt alone.

For, despite the many opportunities surrounding him, David never felt comfortable in the palace. He was surprised to find that the rush of excitement he experienced upon accepting Samuel's anointing back home had failed to repeat itself here in Gibeah. And though David did what he could to find that feeling again, his thoughts continually drifted back to the hills of Bethlehem and the flock he had left behind—as though they were calling him home.

～

Scriptures influencing this chapter:

· 1 Samuel 16:23 – David plays for Saul when he is tormented.

CHAPTER

SEVENTEEN

REALIZATION

*"The Lord makes firm the steps of the one who delights
in him; though he may stumble, he will not fall, for the
Lord upholds him with his hand."*
—Psalm 37:23–24

As the weeks turned into months, David could not avoid seeing the trouble growing in the palace. What had once seemed like a place of grandeur and strength now revealed itself as something far more fragile. Beneath its polished surface, a creeping darkness spread, tightening its grip on all who walked the halls.

David watched how Saul ruled with an iron fist, his presence casting a shadow over every corridor. His sharp voice left no room for dissent, his piercing gaze searching for threats where none existed. Servants flinched at the sound of his voice, unsure whether their next movement would earn them praise or punishment. Advisors did not seek wisdom but survival, choosing the counsel they gave not by what was right, but by what was the most safe.

Although Saul had once inspired loyalty, he now ruled through fear. It spread like weeds in a garden, curling around every heart, strangling trust, and turning men against one another in desperate self-preservation. Where there should have been strength in a common purpose, Saul had created a world of bitter distrust. Indeed, the old proverb was true: "As the head turns, so follows the body."

David could feel it pressing in on him. He had no enemies in the palace, yet he constantly felt uneasy. He found his thoughts continually drifting back to the hills of Bethlehem, to the open fields and the quiet steadiness of his flock. He thought coming to the palace would bring him closer to his destiny, but now, standing in the heart of Israel's power, he felt further away than ever.

As David wandered the halls one day, thinking about the delicate situation he now found himself in, he came upon Hophas sitting in an alcove by himself. David approached slowly, hoping not to startle the king's advisor who seemed lost in thought.

"Good morning Hophas, I'm sorry to bother you." he said as the advisor looked up to see him approaching.

Hophas always had a smile that was open and inviting, which was a refreshing contrast to most of Saul's advisors.

"Good morning, David. It is no bother at all, please sit. How are you doing? You seem to be fitting in with life here in the palace."

David hesitated before sitting beside him. "Can I speak plainly with you?"

"Always." Hophas said, his expression attentive.

David leaned in closer, hoping to avoid anybody overhearing their conversation. "I'm starting to wonder whether I should have come to the palace or not."

Now Hophas also looked around to make sure nobody was listening in. "David, I know the palace is a different life than where you are from, but you were summoned to come here by the king himself. That is not a small thing. Very few people will ever have such an opportunity in their lifetime."

David nodded his head. "I know, and I am grateful for the opportunity. Truly. When you came with the summons, it felt like a sign—an open door I had to walk through. But the longer I'm here, the more it feels like I stepped through the wrong one. I've been here for months and still feel like a stranger. Does that make any sense?"

Hophas studied him for a moment before replying. "I'm sure this has been difficult for you. You are young and you've left behind everything you've ever known to come here. Maybe you just need more time."

David shifted uncomfortably. "There's something I

never told you." he said, lowering his voice. "The day you arrived with the summons... I heard a voice in the wind telling me to stay with my sheep. I think it was the Lord. But I ignored it."

David searched Hophas' face for a reaction, worried that he sounded crazy, but his gaze was met only with kindness and understanding. After a brief pause, Hophas responded gently.

"Sometimes the Lord speaks but we don't yet know how to listen. And sometimes, we must take the wrong path to learn how to recognize the right one."

David looked questioningly at Hophas, unsure of what he meant.

Hophas continued, "The Lord's voice isn't always the loudest one. It often whispers and therefore gets drowned out by our own thoughts. But that whisper still leaves a mark on the heart. If peace has been hard to find here, maybe that whisper was meant to guide you to something you couldn't yet understand."

David's brow furrowed. "So, what do I do now? I made the choice to come here to the palace. What if it was the wrong one?"

Hophas placed a hand on his shoulder. "Listen closely, David; Wrong paths can still lead to right places when we walk them with humility. If something inside you remains restless, it's not punishment—it's the Lord nudging you in a different direction. Don't be afraid to turn back. Some paths are only meant to teach us what our true journey feels like."

David frowned. "If the voice I ignored really was the Lord trying to stop me, then I'm afraid I am just as lost as King Saul. Now the Lord knows He can't trust me to listen to His voice."

Hophas considered David's words for a moment before responding. "Or maybe the Lord knew you would take this step—even needed you to take it. Not because it was perfect, but because it would teach you something no pasture or sheep ever could. Important lessons can be learned from our mistakes if we stay humble. Some paths are not meant to carry you all the way to your destiny. Some are simply meant to prepare your feet to walk the one that does."

David looked out across the hallway, the stone floor stretching before him. "But how do I know when to turn back or when to leave the path I'm on?"

Hophas tilted his head. "When the path begins to silence your soul instead of stirring it. When your spirit feels like a guest instead of a guide. That's when you pause and ask again, 'Lord, is this where you still want me?'"

David sat in thoughtful silence.

Hophas added, "Whatever choice you've made, you are not behind, and you are not off course. You are learning. And the Lord is not standing at the finish line shaking His head and waiting for you to get it right, He's walking beside you; even on the road that turns back."

David let the words settle. "So even if I made a mistake, He can still use it for my benefit?"

Hophas nodded. "He always does. Just don't let pride keep you from returning to the fields if that's where He's calling you. Some of the greatest journeys begin when we have the courage to go back to where we first heard His voice."

THAT NIGHT, David slipped away from the candlelit corridors and climbed the narrow stairs to the rooftop. The city of Gibeah lay quiet below, bathed in moonlight, but his heart felt anything but still. He came here looking for guidance, just as he had when he climbed his rooftop back home to speak with Samuel.

He knelt beside the stone wall, the cool wind brushing against his face.

Clasping his hands, he whispered into the open sky, "Lord... I don't know the way."

His voice cracked.

"I wanted to follow You. I really did. But when the summons came, I stopped listening. I thought the palace was the next step. I thought... maybe this was the path to what Samuel anointed me for."

He paused, searching the stars for an answer that didn't come.

"I understand now that it was Your voice in the wind, and I ignored it. I feared being left behind. I feared missing my moment. And for that... I am sorry."

The silence stretched around him, but this time it did

not hold loneliness or fear, it just held space, allowing David to experience the moment.

He bowed his head lower. "What should I do now?"

David waited in silence, but there was no reply.

No voice.

No vision.

Only stillness.

But in that stillness, something shifted.

The turmoil in his mind settled. A calmness permeated through his body, as though the wind itself had wrapped around his soul and whispered, "You already know what you should do."

David opened his eyes and exhaled deeply. Not with total certainty, but with peace.

He felt the answer in his heart.

It was time to go home.

EIGHTEEN

THE MINOR FALL

"Though I stumble, I will not fall,
for the Lord upholds me with his hand."
—Psalm 37:24

Late the next evening, David was once again summoned to play for the king. He found Saul sitting alone in the throne room, deep in thought. David took his usual spot in the corner of the room and began to play. As he did, he saw the king's shoulders slowly relax as they always did. The feeling in the room became more calm and less frantic.

As David played the calming melody, he didn't notice that the king's eyes were set upon him, a thoughtful and calculating expression on his face. Saul had not forgotten the feeling he had when first meeting the shepherd. And though the moment had raised some questions in his mind, he had never explored them further.

After listening to the music for a while, the king spoke: "Why did you come here to my palace?"

David was startled and looked around to see who else was in the room. The king rarely spoke to David directly unless dismissing him.

"I came because you summoned me to play for you," David replied timidly.

"Indeed, and your talent is greatly appreciated. You have not told me much about your life before coming here. Tell me what you left behind to be in my service."

David wasn't sure exactly how to answer. The king had never shown any interest in him outside of his abilities with the harp. But he paused for a moment to think back to his home.

"I didn't really leave much behind. Just my family and my sheep." he finally responded.

Saul was amused. "It doesn't sound like much. Was it hard to leave?"

David reflected briefly, "I'm the youngest in my family, and my brothers were never very kind to me. To be honest, it was harder to leave my sheep."

Saul chuckled softly. "I know the feeling. Before I was called to be the king, I was in charge of my father's animals as well."

"Really?" David said in amazement. "How did you become king?"

"It was strange," Saul said. "I was out with my friends

searching for my father's lost animals. We came across an old prophet named Samuel and thought maybe he could help us find them. Before I knew it, I was anointed to be king of all Israel. He told me I had been chosen by the Lord to lead the people."

David was astonished by the similarities between Saul's story and his own experience with Samuel. He thought it wise not to share this with the king, however. David shuttered at the thought of what would happen if he told the mighty Saul that he would one day replace him on the throne.

"That is an amazing story," replied David. Then, reflecting his own thoughts, added, "It must be both extraordinary and humbling to be chosen by the Lord."

The king paused as the memory came to his mind. "Honestly, it was terrifying at first. I tried to run from it and hide. I felt like Samuel had made a mistake."

David fully understood the feelings Saul was expressing and looked to give the king the support he wished he had received from his brothers.

"But you are one of the strongest men in all of Israel. You are a great warrior. You are exactly the king we all wanted. I don't believe there was a mistake."

Saul laughed bitterly. "All of those achievements, and still, they are never enough. No matter what I do, it seems someone is always displeased. Samuel is never satisfied. When I defeat my enemies, he claims I acted in haste. When I wait for the right moment, the people call me indecisive. No matter what I do, someone will call me a tyrant, and someone else a fool."

As Saul sat in silent contemplation, David found himself empathizing with the king for the first time. He understood how hard it could be to listen to the voice of the Lord when so many other voices spoke more loudly; he himself was guilty of the same mistake. David felt a flicker of guilt for being chosen to replace a king who was struggling with the same thing he was.

Looking to support the king as much as possible, David broke the silence. "Although it is difficult, I know that both the Lord and Samuel will help you lead our people. There will always be those who don't like the decisions you make, but you must be strong and do what your heart tells you is right. The Lord will always help you if you trust Him."

Saul looked up, feeling somewhat lifted by the hopeful words of the young musician. He studied David for a few moments and as he did, something stirred within him again. There was definitely something about this boy that he couldn't quite describe, and it made Saul feel uneasy. "I need to keep this one close," he thought to himself.

He turned from his thoughts and addressed David directly. "You are a remarkable young man. Your wisdom surpasses that of men twice your age, and your insight is rare. I think it is time for you to step beyond the role of court musician. I want you to become my armor bearer. You will accompany me in all matters, learning the art of war and the strategies of leadership. Here in the palace, you will live a life of luxury, with opportunities to rise as an advisor to the king, or even a general in the army. You need never return to the fields or your flock. Your life is about to transform in ways you could never have imagined."

Saul leaned back on his throne, satisfaction spreading across his face as he considered the honor he had just bestowed upon David. Elevating a humble shepherd to such heights surely was an act of greatness.

Yet, something felt unsettled. David stood motionless, his gaze distant, as though the importance of the king's words had not yet reached him. He didn't appear joyful or eager, as Saul had expected.

Saul's eyes narrowed as he observed the young man further, waiting for a response.

David's mind was a whirlwind of thoughts. Serving the king, learning the ways of war—every logical part of his brain was once again screaming that this was the path to the destiny Samuel had foretold. The pieces were falling into place too perfectly to be anything else. Maybe his decision to go home was made too hastily.

But even as his mind urged him to accept, his heart once again tugged him in another direction. Had he not felt an overwhelming peace in his heart when he made the decision to return home, the first time he had felt that way in months? And the voice he had heard in the wind on the day he left home was no mere whisper of doubt— he was certain of that now—it had been the voice of the

Lord. Somehow, the palace and all its opportunities could never teach him the lessons waiting for him in the hills back home. The honor of serving as Saul's armor bearer clashed sharply with the humble path the Lord had set for him.

David struggled with the nervous energy in his body as he wrestled with his thoughts.

Saul's impatient voice pulled David back to the present.

"Well, what do you say? Are you ready to leave that lowly shepherd life behind for good and join me here in the palace?"

David looked up and began to speak, his words almost failing to leave his lips.

"My king, you have bestowed upon me a great honor, and I am humbled that you find me worthy of such a place at your side. But I cannot stay. I have a responsibility to my family and my sheep back home. I do not feel that I am meant to leave them right now. I am grateful that you brought me here and for this honor you bestow upon me, but I feel the Lord's spirit telling me I need to go home. I hope you understand."

Saul's smile vanished, replaced by a storm of fury that surged through him like fire. His face flushed, and his hands clenched tightly as rage overtook him.

"The spirit of the Lord told you this? Have you lost your mind?" he bellowed, his voice echoing through the throne room. "Who are you to defy your king's command? I was chosen by the Lord to rule over all Israel, and yet you—a mere shepherd boy—dare to presume you know better? You are nothing but a peasant, and I offered to make you great! And still, you insult me by choosing your pathetic sheep over your king. Such insolence deserves nothing but death!"

Without hesitation, Saul seized a spear resting against the wall and hurled it with all his might, aiming for David's heart. Instinctively, David twisted to the side, the spear slicing through his tunic but missing its mark. It struck a wooden dish resting on a nearby table, shattering it and scattering its contents across the stone floor.

Saul advanced, his face twisted with rage as he grabbed the sword hanging on the wall. David backed away, his pulse racing, and as Saul surged forward, David turned and fled. His feet raced over the cold stone floor as he tried to escape but, as he neared the doorway, his foot suddenly slipped on something smooth, sending him sprawling forward to the ground.

David landed hard among the scattered contents of the broken dish: precious stones, smooth and polished, that gleamed around him on the ground.

One stone, dark and lustrous, caught his gaze.

Time slowed almost to a stop as he felt compelled to reach for it. As he did, his own reflection flickered on its surface for an instant, then shifted.

Now he saw his flock, grazing on the hillside outside of Bethlehem. They milled about peacefully, but in the distance, something moved. From the tall grass, a lion emerged. David's heart tightened. He knew that form—every muscle, every stride. It was the lion. The one that had taken his sheep. The one that had paralyzed him with fear. The one whose roar still haunted his dreams.

But this time, the lion did not strike the flock. It paused. Then slowly, it turned its massive head and locked eyes with David through the surface of the stone. Its piercing gaze seemed to say, "You remember me. And I remember you. I'll always be here waiting for you."

David could not look away. He could feel his heart beating wildly as the lion finally broke its gaze and turned back towards the flock, crouching low in the grass, waiting to pounce.

As the scene unfolded, David suddenly heard a familiar voice echo deep within him: "How many? "

Just two words— yet they pierced David like a knife to his soul. Not with pain for himself, but for his flock back home. A surge of love rose within him and in that instant, he understood clearly that the Lord was teaching him a deeper lesson:

To protect what he loved, to stand between danger and the innocent... this was his true calling for now. Leadership would not begin with a throne—it would begin by finding the courage to defend the helpless.

The palace would have to wait.

There was a fear he needed to face on a hillside back home.

Saul's enraged screams jolted David back to the

moment. Grasping the black stone, he scrambled to his feet and bolted through the doorway, narrowly evading the swing of Saul's blade. He ran through the courtyard, the echoes of Saul's wrath following him as he fled into the city.

At the doorway, Saul stood, sword in hand, his voice rising to a roar. "You will regret this, boy! You could have had everything, but now you will amount to nothing! Mark my words, David—you will die in obscurity with your sheep. You are nothing, and you will always be nothing!"

SCRIPTURES INFLUENCING THIS CHAPTER:

- 1 Samuel 9 – The story of Saul's calling.
- 1 Samuel 16:21 – David named Saul's armor bearer.
- 1 Samuel 18:10-11 – Saul tries to kill David with a spear.

CHAPTER

NINETEEN

A SHEPHERD'S RETURN

"The Lord is close to the brokenhearted
and saves those who are crushed in spirit."
—Psalm 34:18

David's footsteps echoed faintly on the rocky trail as he made his way from Gibeah; the light of the moon was all he had to illuminate the path. He clenched the black stone from Saul's palace tightly in his hand. The sting of Saul's bitter words still hung in the air, but David's heart was steadied by something far deeper. Although he was walking in the darkness of night, he felt a light kindled within him.

"How strange." he thought to himself as the lights of Gibeah grew smaller in the distance. "I'm walking away from the palace, but I feel closer to my destiny. Hophas was right—sometimes the wrong path teaches us how to recognize the right one."

The thought drew his memory back to the words Samuel shared when they first met on the road outside of Bethlehem, "If you feel destined for something greater, learn to master what is before you."

David felt a pang of sorrow for ever resenting the shepherd's role. His brothers had all begun there—why should he be different? The voice of the man in the stables echoed in his mind: "How you do anything is how you do everything. When you are faithful in the small things, the Lord blesses you with bigger things."

As he walked with his thoughts, David began to realize that it wasn't entirely about the sheep—it was about trust. The Lord wanted to see if David could master small tasks before being entrusted with greater ones. How could he lead a nation if he hadn't learned to protect a flock? How could he follow the Lord's commands if he hadn't fully learned how to recognize His voice?

By the time David reached Bethlehem, the early dawn light was stretching across the fields. Familiar sounds and smells reached his senses, though he was still lost in thought as he made his way home. Approaching the courtyard, David spotted his mother in the doorway of the house. When she saw him, a look of astonishment and excitement crossed her face. She ran and greeted him at the gate, wrapping him in a tight embrace full of both relief and concern.

"I am so happy you are home. You must have traveled all night, are you okay?"

Before David could answer he heard footsteps coming near and looked up. Jesse had come from the house to see what had caused the commotion and was startled to see his son back from the palace.

"David, you're back," Jesse said in a stern and questioning voice. "What happened? Why did you leave the king's court? Do you realize what this could mean for your future?"

David hesitated, "Father, it... it wasn't the right time. I wasn't supposed to be there. I know it seems foolish, but the Lord's voice was clear. The time to serve as a king will come, but not yet."

Neither of his parents responded and as the silence drew on, David began to weep. "I've made a mistake and now I fear I have lost the Lord's favor. I haven't heard His voice since leaving home. I tried to do it my way and I failed. I've wasted so much time."

Nitzevet grabbed the sides of her son's head with both hands and brought it up until she was looking straight into his eyes. "David, you have not failed." she said tenderly. "The Lord's ways are beyond our understanding and His plans are not undone by human missteps. He sees the greater tapestry of our lives and he knows how each thread is woven with purpose —even the threads we wish we could undo. Whatever choices you've made, they were never outside the reach of His plan for you. You haven't fallen behind. You are exactly where He needs you to be, because you've grown along the way."

David stared lovingly into his mother's eyes and then bowed his head. "Thank you, Mother. I will try to remember that going forward. Right now, I could use some food and a bed."

As they walked toward the house, Jesse began to protest, eager for more answers. But a firm glance from Nitzevet silenced him, signaling that the discussion would have to wait.

~

SCRIPTURES INFLUENCING THIS CHAPTER:

· 1 Samuel 17:15 – David returns to Bethlehem

TWENTY

REFLECTION

"Search me, O God, and know my heart;
test me and know my anxious thoughts."
—Psalm 139:23

When David awoke later in the day, the house was quiet and empty. He dressed quickly and set out, eager to find his sheep. It wasn't long before he spotted them near the familiar tree where he had spent so many days. But his heart sank when he noticed the figure standing watch over the flock —Eliab, his eldest brother. David could only imagine how reluctantly Eliab must have agreed to their father's request to tend the sheep in his absence, a task far beneath his station in his own eyes.

"I knew you'd be back," Eliab said tersely, his voice sharp and disapproving. "I thought you'd found a better life in the palace. What are you doing here?"

David paused, unsure what words to use that would both help his brother understand and avoid the inevitable mockery that would come. "The sheep need me," he said simply. "There is something I still need to learn here."

Eliab scoffed, shaking his head. "So, you failed and now you're coming back here to your sheep? Seems fitting for someone only playing at being a king. The palace must not have thought much of you to send you crawling back here." He thrust the staff toward David with a sneer and then walked off, leaving him alone with the flock.

David didn't know how to respond in a way that his brother or anyone would understand. To them, his return was proof of failure. He was still the little brother who dared to dream too big.

The sheep milled around, their bleats rising and falling like a soft, familiar melody. As David stepped among them, a sense of peace began to settle over him. He looked lovingly at his flock and felt a wave of regret swell within him. He should have listened to the Lord's voice, the gentle urging to stay. Leaving the sheep had seemed like the right path, but now he realized it had been an abandonment of the lessons the Lord still wanted him to learn here.

David leaned on his staff, looking out at the familiar surroundings that stretched before him. He whispered sadly to himself, "Here I am again, right where I started. I pushed for my own plan and timing—and I failed."

Reaching into his pouch, David pulled out the polished black stone he had brought from Saul's palace. He turned it over in his hand, its smooth surface cool against his palm. The memory of his flight from the palace flashed vividly in his mind—the tension in the throne room, the fire of Saul's fury, the desperate scramble to escape. The nighttime journey back to Bethlehem had brought a mixture of both peace and self-doubt, which raised some troubling questions: Had he lost the Lord's blessing just like Saul? Was he still called to be the king of Israel?

David closed his eyes, hoping the soft breeze drifting across the hills might carry some kind of answer. But this time the wind gave no reply—only silence. His thoughts spun in circles, reaching for something steady to cling to, but no comfort came.

After a while, he let out a long breath and stopped trying to think his way through it. Hophas had once told him, "The mind wrestles for control but the heart holds the truth." So David tried to silence his thoughts and focus on what his heart was saying.

At first, there was only stillness. No voice, no stirring in his heart. But he remained there patiently, determined to find answers. Gradually, as he leaned into the silence, something deeper began to rise—not answers, but better questions. Questions that didn't come from fear or doubt, but from a place of truth.

What if Hophas and his mother were right, and he had not failed?

What if stumbling isn't the same as falling?

What if the Lord is still writing my story, even in the chapters I wish didn't exist?

"A misstep or bad decision might slow the journey, but it doesn't have to end it," he thought. "Maybe our falls help us see the Lord's path more clearly because they bend our knees, lift our eyes, and quiet our pride. Perhaps it is in the messiness of our mistakes that we learn to hear the Lord more clearly. Saul didn't lose the Lord's favor because he made mistakes, it was because he was lifted so high up in pride and power that he became blind to the path the Lord was guiding him to."

David's gaze shifted to the horizon, where the hills stretched endlessly into the distance. Perhaps his time in the palace—including the discomfort, the doubt, even the moments of fear—was not wasted. Each of those experiences had taught him something, even if the lessons had only just begun to take root in his heart.

David traced the edges of the stone with his thumb, letting the thought settle. "This stone was made smooth by the grit of the tools that polished it, applied by the loving hands of a craftsman. Perhaps the Lord uses the roughness of our struggles and missteps to polish us into something more valuable."

David took another deep, calming breath and looked again at his familiar surroundings. This place, once a reminder of his supposed failure, now felt like a training ground—a place where the Lord was preparing him, not despite his struggles, but through them.

"I will stumble again," he whispered, "I'm sure of it. But each time, I'll rise stronger. The Lord does not waste the falls, He uses them to teach us how to walk. I will keep this stone to remind me to get back up when I am knocked down. A fall is only a failure if I don't get back up. I will look to this stone to help me persevere through the hard times on my journey and remember that the Lord is using them to polish me into something more valuable."

David paused, then pulled another stone from his pouch, this time it was the red-colored stone Samuel had given him, the stone that represented vision.

"These two stones together will be a source of strength for me. The vision to see who I am meant to become combined with the determination to persevere when the journey gets difficult is a powerful combination."

With that said, David returned the stones to his pouch, and his gaze to the sheep grazing around him. "Now," he said, "let's see what the Lord has prepared for me."

TWENTY-ONE

COURAGE

*"Wait for the Lord; be strong,
and let your heart take courage;
wait for the Lord!"*
—Psalm 27:14

David rose early the next day and led his flock to the fields, just as he had before leaving for Gibeah. As the sheep grazed, he leaned on his staff, reflecting on how much they had grown in the months he was gone. Lambs that had once needed constant attention now moved confidently among the flock.

"Mother said that I am exactly where I am supposed to be. What more can my sheep possibly teach me?" he wondered.

As the day gave way to the warmth of the afternoon, David settled under the shade of his olive tree and closed his eyes. The gentle hum of the wind sweeping through the grass lulled him to sleep, but his rest was short-lived.

A sudden, panicked bleating jolted him awake. David scrambled to his feet, scanning the flock. The sheep were scattering in all directions, making it hard for him to find the source of the panic. His eyes finally focused on a thick concentration of bushes halfway up the hill. His heart dropped as he saw an enormous shape emerging from the thicket, a lamb struggling helplessly in its jaws.

The lion had come.

It had been waiting for one of the sheep to wander close enough to its hiding spot before attacking.

Instinctively, David reached for his sling and a handful of stones from his pouch, but fear gripped him once again. He was frozen in place for just a moment. But summoning all his strength and courage, he broke free.

"Not again!" he yelled as he frantically slotted a stone and began swinging. He let it go, but being overwhelmed by panic, he released the stone too soon. His shot whistled harmlessly over the lion, who scarcely noticed the stone flying past.

David took a breath to try to calm himself as he slotted another stone. Focusing on his target and swinging his sling faster and faster, he released a second shot. This time it hit, striking the beast in the side, eliciting a growl that made David's blood run cold. The lion turned, dropping the lamb, and fixed its fierce eyes on him; just as it had in the image on the stone.

The moment had come.

The crossroads.

The reason the Lord had called him back home.

David's instinct screamed at him to flee, to save himself and the rest of the flock. Yet, something stronger held him in place—a voice—clear, steady, and resolute:

"Stand firm, David. Protect what has been entrusted to you. Fear has no place here; I am with you."

He recognized the voice of the Lord this time, and the words sent a sensation through his body, filling him with a courage that burned brighter than his fear.

The lion charged, its massive frame bearing down on him. David fumbled for another stone but his pouch tipped, spilling the remaining stones onto the rocky ground. Desperation clawed at him as he dropped to his knees, his hands frantically searching through the dirt while his eyes darted between the scattered stones and the advancing lion.

His fingers closed around a rock—not one of his smooth slinging stones, but a rough, jagged stone lying in the grass. It would have to do. Without hesitation, he slotted it into his sling and began to swing.

The lion surged forward with terrifying speed, covering the distance between them in no time. David held his ground, but just as he prepared to release the stone, the beast barreled into him, its weight slamming him to the earth. Pain ripped through his side as he hit the ground, the impact driving the air from his lungs. Gasping, David tried to crawl backward, his hands scrambling for purchase on the loose ground, but the lion loomed above him, letting out a roar that shook the very hillside.

Desperation gripped David as he fumbled for the knife at his belt. The lion's blood-stained teeth glinted menacingly as it prepared for the final attack, its enormous frame blotting out the light. David's fingers finally found the knife handle and, drawing on every ounce of strength he had left, he thrust upward wildly with his blade just as the beast lunged for his throat.

The lion's roar of fury was replaced by a cry of pain as David's blade found its mark. The knife sank deep into the lion's chest, its final, ferocious cry reverberating through the hills. The great beast held for a moment, its face just inches away from David's. Their eyes met one last time and then the lion stumbled, its massive body falling heavily beside David, the ground trembling with its weight.

Breathing hard, David lay on the ground, his mind racing and his body trembling. He had done it. In the face of certain death he had found the courage to fight back to protect those he loved.

As the world began to calm, a soft bleating drew him back to the present moment. Rising unsteadily, he saw the lamb he had saved limping towards him. Tears began to form as David cradled it in his arms and buried his face in its fur, its tiny body trembling but alive.

As he carried the lamb back to the flock, blood streaking his tunic, he found his sling with the brown, jagged rock lying next to it. A new certainty settled over him as he  picked up the stone and examined its rough and imperfect surface. "I could have run. I could have frozen again. But in the moment, all that mattered was that I decided to do something even when I was scared. Courage is not the absence of fear but the decision to act in spite of it. That's what saved the flock. That's what saved me."

"I will carry this stone as a reminder to always act in the face of fear, even when facing the unknown. This stone is rough and imperfect, just as I am. But the Lord doesn't need me to be perfect, He just needs me to be willing."

Scanning the hillside to locate the rest of his scattered flock, David's mind reflected further on the lesson he had learned. The same courage needed to defend his flock would also be needed to defend his dreams. This hillside was exactly where he needed to be to learn that valuable lesson. He shook his head and gave a small chuckle as he recognized the Lord's wisdom in his journey.

"I understand now," he said, his mind gaining new clarity, "I am exactly where I am supposed to be, to learn what I am supposed to learn, to become who I am supposed to become. The Lord led me back to the exact place I needed to be to learn how to move forward."

David leaned back against the tree, his body aching,

and whispered a quiet prayer of gratitude. He didn't know the full path ahead, but he felt one step closer to under-standing what it truly meant to be a shepherd—and a king.

Scriptures influencing this chapter:

· 1 Samuel 17:34– David talks about killing the lion.

CHAPTER

TWENTY-TWO

PREPARATION

"He trains my hands for battle;
my arms can bend a bow of bronze."
—Psalm 18:34

In the weeks that followed, David fell back into the familiar rhythm of tending the flock yet, this time, everything felt different. He no longer saw the hills of Bethlehem as a place of exile but as a classroom.

"When the Lord calls me to lead, I must be ready. This is where He wants me to be, so I cannot waste this time I have been given to prepare," he said one day as he walked home from the fields.

As he had done in the palace, David looked for opportunities to learn. He began spending more time in town, eager to hear the wisdom of the village Elders. Although they all remembered the prophet Samuel's visit and David's anointing, most of them gave the shepherd no consideration. One of the Elders however, a scribe named Malchiah, eventually took notice of David's persistent visits.

"You return often, young shepherd," Malchiah said one afternoon, setting aside a scroll he was copying. "Why do you seek the knowledge of old men when there are hills to roam and sheep to tend?"

David hesitated before answering. "Do you remember when Samuel came to Bethlehem? He told me then that the Lord has called me to something greater, but I'm still not ready. I need to learn—about leadership, about battle, and about how to protect people—and I need to learn quickly because the Lord could call at any moment."

Malchiah studied him before nodding. "Wisdom is a noble goal, but it rarely comes quickly, David. It is built slowly, like a wall—each stone carefully laid upon the one before it. If you try to place the capstone without working on the foundation, everything will crumble. You have chosen to follow the Lord's path, but you don't get to dictate His timing. The Lord will call when the time is right, until then, keep building your foundation."

David pondered Malchiah's words as he walked home, and they reminded him of his decision to have patience in the learning process.

He thought again of the days spent with his flock—searching for lost sheep, standing watch against predators, and tending to the sick. These tasks had once felt so small and insignificant, but now he knew they were essential.

Every moment spent caring for his flock was like a stone added to the wall of his preparation to one day lead Israel. That capstone may still be far off, but Malchiah's words reminded him that it could not stand without the strength of the foundation that came first.

As if by divine guidance, David's path took him past a crumbling stone wall, its original purpose long lost to memory. The weathered stones, once carefully placed, now lay scattered on the ground, their edges softened by years of wind and rain.

David paused, then crouched to pick up one of the smaller stones. It fit easily in his hand, its surface cool and smooth, a quiet reminder of how even something strong, like this wall,  could falter without care and attention. He turned the stone over in his hand as he reflected on the lesson he had learned from Malchiah.

"The capstone will come," he said quietly, his gaze sweeping over the hills. "But for now, I will focus on the foundation. This stone will remind me that greatness doesn't happen in an instant, it is built day by day, stone by stone."

He smiled faintly as he slipped the stone into his pouch and continued walking down the path.

~

DAY AFTER DAY, David continued to dedicate his free time to learning wherever he could. He turned curiosity into an art, as the washerwoman had once counseled, asking questions of anyone he could learn from. He worked alongside craftsmen, learning the intricacies of building and the importance of creating with care. He spent time with the town's scribes, who taught him the art of writing and speaking with precision. All of Bethlehem became his classroom and every inhabitant, his teacher.

The flock, ever his constant companions, became his practice for leadership. He learned to anticipate their needs, to guide them with both gentleness and firmness. When one sheep strayed, he learned how to bring it back without alarming the others. When predators lurked, he honed his strategies to prevent an attack, thereby protecting the flock with minimal risk to himself and the animals.

The more he learned and practiced, the more confident David became. He could feel the excitement of momentum turning in his favor, propelling him closer to the purpose he was meant to fulfill.

The people in town noticed as well, showing eagerness to help him where they could. Though they lacked the words to describe it, they felt the energy and inspiration that always radiates from a person working toward their destiny.

His older brothers, however, watched his efforts with thinly veiled disdain. David had grown so much over the past year, but they still only saw him as a boy with dreams beyond his abilities. Their mocking words still hurt, even though David knew they shouldn't. He understood that some people resent those who chase their destiny because it forces them to examine their own unfilled potential. But even with that understanding, being rejected by family hurt in ways that nothing else could.

Six months turned into a year. David's days were filled with purpose, and his nights were spent in reflection under the stars. The stone Samuel had given him over a year ago remained in his pouch, joined by the others he had collected along the way as constant reminders of the path he was on. Though the journey was far from over, he felt himself growing into the man he was meant to be. And as the seasons shifted, the boy who had once doubted his calling began to disappear, replaced by someone stronger, wiser, and more prepared.

CHAPTER

TWENTY-THREE

THE CALL TO BATTLE

"I trust in you, Lord;
I say, 'You are my God.'
My times are in your hands."
—Psalm 31:14–15

The messenger arrived at dawn, his voice echoing through the quiet streets of Bethlehem. "The Philistines march against Israel! King Saul calls for soldiers to defend the land!" The cry sent ripples through the village, breaking the calm of the morning. Fathers, sons, and brothers gathered in small clusters, murmuring in low tones about the looming battle.

At Jesse's house, the news hit like a thunderclap. Eliab, Abinadab, and Shammah were already preparing, their excitement barely concealed as they strapped on

145

their gear and spoke in hurried tones. Their faces showed determination, though beneath their bravado lay the nervous energy of men heading into the unknown.

David watched from the corner of the room, his heart sinking. He had overheard the messenger's proclamation and felt the familiar stir of excitement in his chest. Yet even before his father spoke, he knew what was coming.

"Eliab, Abinadab, Shammah," Jesse said, his voice firm but warm. "You are the oldest. You will go to the battlefield to fight for Israel and for our king." His gaze shifted to David, softening. "But you, my son, will stay with the rest of your brothers. The farm needs tending, and the flock cannot be left without care. I need you here."

David's hands clenched into fists at his sides. Although he had committed to trusting the Lord's timing, being left behind again cut deeply, allowing raw emotion to spill out. "But, Father, I can fight!" he demanded. "I've proven that while defending the sheep. You've seen how hard I have been working, let me go with my brothers!"

Eliab turned sharply, his expression darkening. "Fight?" he scoffed. "You're still just a boy, David, no matter what an old prophet said. Do you think the battlefield is like chasing sheep on a hillside? Stay where you belong."

Abinadab chuckled, shaking his head. "Anyway, he'd probably just try to serenade the Philistines with his harp."

David held his ground, his face turning red. "I know how to face danger! I single-handedly killed a lion while protecting our flock; I don't remember any of you doing that. The Lord gave me the strength then, and He will give me strength now."

Jesse placed a hand on David's shoulder, his grip comforting yet firm. "David, take a breath. Your courage is not in question, but your time has not yet come. I know the Lord has called you, but you are still very young. For now, your place is here, to ensure the farm runs smoothly in your brothers' absence. That is no small task."

David's jaw tightened, and as his emotions subsided, he nodded reluctantly. He turned to Eliab, who stood with his chest puffed out, adjusting the straps on his tunic.

"One day," David said quietly, "you'll see that courage isn't determined by size."

Eliab snorted, dismissing his brother with a wave. "We'll see if you're still spouting wisdom when we return as heroes." The other brothers gave a loud cheer in response.

DAVID STOOD ALONE in the doorway watching his brothers disappear down the path through town. The sight brought up old wounds that David thought he had healed from, carrying with them a fresh set of doubts.

He thought he had learned to trust in the Lord's timing; but patience was proving difficult. He had poured himself into preparation, yet it felt as though no one who mattered—not even the Lord—had taken notice.

Questions flooded his mind: Why couldn't his family see the growth that he was experiencing? When would he stop being passed over because of his size? When would the Lord give him a chance?

A hand gently rested on his shoulder and David turned to see his mother standing beside him, her eyes set on the horizon.

"How are you feeling?" she asked tenderly.

David struggled to hide his emotions. "When will my time come?" he replied, his voice quivering. "Does the Lord even see the effort I am making or how much I have grown?"

Nitzevet remained quiet, allowing David a moment to wrestle with his feelings. When it felt right, she lovingly turned to meet his gaze. "It is okay to feel what you are feeling. There are seasons in life when we invest a lot of effort and don't see the results. This can make us doubt ourselves or question the Lord and His promises. But let me ask you this: are you willing to do the work even if the Lord doesn't see it?"

David looked at her with a puzzled expression. "What do you mean?"

She continued, "Are you willing to keep improving yourself —not for recognition, not for reward—but simply because it is the right thing to do? If no one was watching, would you still put in the effort? Because if your answer is 'no', then you may be missing the point of what the Lord expects from you. He isn't looking for someone who does the right thing because they expect recognition,

He is looking for someone who will do the right thing just because it is the right thing to do. Are you willing to do that?"

David thought for a moment and then walked over to the corner of the room where his shepherd's crook and pouch were placed. He reached into the pouch and pulled out the grey stone he had found by the crumbling wall, the stone that represented preparation and self-discipline. He turned it over in his hands in contemplation as he walked back to where his mother stood.

"I found this stone one day and saved it as a reminder to patiently build my own foundation before it was time to become the king. Perhaps I thought my efforts were building a staircase to reach the throne at the top, but maybe that's the wrong way to think about it. Maybe I am building my own palace, day by day, because I already have a king inside of me and true kings build because it is right, not because it is rewarded."

Nitzevet nodded reassuringly and gently closed David's fingers around the stone. "I think you'll find that as soon as you are determined to become your best self for no other reason than to be your best self, the Lord's opportunities will arrive. Can you do that?"

He nodded and they embraced. Gratitude filled his heart for a mother who exuded quiet strength, unshakable faith, and wisdom as deep as the sea.

David decided in that moment that he would continue improving every day; not just for his mother, and not just for the Lord, but because there was honor in striving to be the best he could be. He would stop waiting for his father to recognize his growth, stop yearning for his brothers' respect, and stop looking for rewards from heaven. He would strive to become the best version of himself possible and let the rest happen in its time.

Standing in the doorway, with eyes turned toward the future, peace filled David's heart and with it came a renewed confidence in who he was and who he was becoming.

Scriptures influencing this chapter:

· 1 Samuel 17:13-15 – Jesse's oldest sons leave to fight for Saul. David is left behind.

CHAPTER
TWENTY-FOUR
OPPORTUNITY

"You armed me with strength for battle;
you humbled my adversaries before me."
—Psalm 18:39

Days stretched into weeks without any word coming from the battlefield. Jesse grew restless, pacing the courtyard every day as he glanced toward the horizon. Surely by now a battle had been fought, why was there no news?

Late one afternoon, as Jesse once again looked out to the hills, he spotted David returning with his flock. As he watched the boy guiding the sheep down the path, he felt a sudden wave of love and respect wash over him. This boy was called by a prophet to be the king of all Israel, and yet he was still here, obediently carrying out his responsibilities. David had grown; Jesse could see it. Despite all the mockery from his older brothers and the mundane nature of his daily chores, he was becoming a man of learning and a man of God.

At some level, Jesse didn't want to believe it. Although he believed in the words of the prophet Samuel, he was scared that David might fail at what he was called to do, bringing shame upon himself and the family. After all, hadn't he failed the last time he left for the palace?

As he continued watching David draw closer, Jesse felt guilty about his doubting thoughts. Why should he doubt the Lord and His plan; can He not make a king of a shepherd? And why could it not be David, his youngest son? Why is it that the people who know us best have the hardest time believing in what we can become?

As Jesse struggled with his thoughts, a warm afternoon breeze swept through the courtyard and across his face. As it did, Jesse felt something in his heart. It wasn't a voice as much as a sensation that carried a message: Let him go. His time has come.

The message was brief and deliberate, but Jesse was still standing there reflecting on it when David reached the house.

Jesse turned to his son and beckoned him to come closer. "Tomorrow, I want you to take grain, bread, and cheese to your brothers at the battlefield, they are surely in need of supplies. Give them whatever support you can."

David hesitated. "Are you sure you don't want to send

one of the others? I don't think any of them would be excited to tend the sheep for me while I was away."

There was a long moment of silence before Jesse turned to David, tears forming in his eyes. "It is time David. The Lord has told me so in my heart. I've held you back because I was afraid that you might fail, but now I know that your time as a shepherd in our home is at an end. You are ready."

Hearing his father's words did not have the effect David had expected. Instead of excitement, he felt a sudden and unexpected wave of doubt. He had spent so long preparing for this moment yet, now that his opportunity had come, fear gnawed at the edges of his resolve. Finally stepping into the unknown, even for something he had long prepared for, carried an uncertainty he hadn't expected.

"I... I don't feel ready yet. I know that I said I was, but I think I need more time." he admitted sheepishly, giving voice to his growing self-doubt.

Jesse shook his head. "David, no one ever feels fully prepared for greatness, no matter how much they've trained or planned. But when the moment arrives, you must trust yourself and step into the unknown. You have prepared well and now all that remains is to have courage and faith. Greatness awaits those who dare greatly. I don't know what will happen when you get to the battlefront but if you trust yourself and trust in the Lord, you will come out on top. I am so proud of you."

David took a slow breath, letting his father's words

settle within him. His father was right—he had done everything he could to prepare. The rest would require faith.

Looking up, he met his father's gaze, seeing a mixture of love and pride reflected in his misty eyes. With a steady nod, David spoke, his voice quiet but resolute. "I will go."

Without another word, Jesse pulled his son into a strong embrace. Neither spoke; they simply held onto each other—both nervous about what lay ahead, yet firm in the knowledge that this was the path the Lord had set before them.

THE NEXT MORNING, David and his family gathered the supplies into a cart and bid their final farewells. His mother hugged him so tight that he could still feel her strength as he made his way through town and out into the countryside.

"Remember, my son" she had whispered in his ear, "The Lord is weaving you into His great tapestry. Trust Him with all your heart."

David paused at the edge of the village, just as he had the last time he left home. His eyes traced the familiar hills where he had spent his days tending the flock. Memories came flooding back to his mind: the boring days tending sheep, the old traveler on the road, the mockery from his brothers, the victory over the lion, the time spent in prayer and preparation.

In the stillness of the moment, a profound peace settled over him. A voice, familiar and unmistakable, rose within him: "You have been faithful in the small things, David. Now go, and I will make you victorious over greater things. The time has come."

A warmth spread through his chest, dissolving any traces of fear that remained. He closed his eyes, breathing deeply, letting the words flood his soul.

The distant bleating of sheep drifted to him on the breeze, a sound that had been the backdrop of his entire life. This was the last time he would walk these hills as their shepherd. Everything would be different moving forward.

David turned toward the road, gripping his staff with newfound confidence. In the quiet of his soul, David made a covenant: he would trust the Lord with everything he was and everything he would become. And the Lord, seeing his heart, knew He could trust David in the challenges that were yet to come.

The shepherd of Bethlehem was ready to become the hero of Israel.

SCRIPTURES INFLUENCING THIS CHAPTER:

· 1 Samuel 17:17-20 – Jesse sends David to the battlefield.

CHAPTER

TWENTY-FIVE

THE CHALLENGE

"The Lord is with me;
I will not be afraid.
What can mere mortals do to me?"
—Psalm 118:6

David found his brothers near the edge of the camp. They were seated with other soldiers, their expressions grim. Eliab spotted David first, rising to his feet with a scowl.

"What are you doing here, David?" he snapped. "Why aren't you bravely defending your sheep?"

David set down the supplies and ignored the jab. "Father sent me with food and to see how I could help. What's happening here? Why does everyone look so defeated?"

Just before Eliab could respond, a deep, thunderous voice boomed across the valley, silencing the camp. David turned toward the sound, his eyes widening as he saw a massive figure step forward from the Philistine lines. The soldier loomed like a mountain, his armor gleaming in the sun. He raised a sword larger than any David had ever seen, pointing it toward the Israelite camp.

"I defy the armies of Israel!" the giant bellowed. "Send a man to fight me! If he kills me, we will become your servants. But if I kill him, you will serve us. Let us see whose God is mightier! Who among you dares to face me?"

David watched as a ripple of fear coursed through the camp. Men began retreating, their eyes downcast, muttering excuses as they moved away. David's brothers exchanged uneasy glances; their earlier bravado gone.

"Who is this Philistine?" David asked, his voice steady despite the tension around him. "How can he stand against the armies of the living God?"

One of the soldiers nearby turned to David, shaking his head. "That's Goliath, the champion of Gath. They say he is unbeatable. He's challenged us every day for weeks, but no one dares face him. The king has promised riches and even his daughter's hand in marriage for the man who defeats him. But who could stand against such a giant?"

David's brow furrowed; his gaze fixed on Goliath. "How does he dare to insult the Lord and His people?"

Eliab's face hardened as he stepped closer to David.

"What do you know, prideful boy?" he hissed. "Why did you come here? To gawk at real warriors and pretend to be important? Go back where you belong!"

David met his brother's glare, his voice calm but confident. "You know what I have been called to do. You know what I am to become. The Lord promises His people victory if they have faith in Him. If you aren't willing to fight for the Lord, then step aside and let me do it."

Eliab was struck silent, the certainty in David's voice cutting through his mockery like a blade.

David turned to the crowd that had formed, speaking more boldly. "Men of Israel, who is this Philistine that dares to mock the armies of the Lord? If the Lord is truly with us, then how can this man stand against us?"

As David scanned the crowd, his gaze unwavering, men lowered their heads, unable to meet his eyes. His words had exposed the fear in their hearts, casting a harsh light on their doubt. This young boy, armed only with his faith, towered above them all, not by stature, but by the strength of his belief in the Lord's power.

SCRIPTURES INFLUENCING THIS CHAPTER:

· 1 Samuel 17:21-27 – David arrives at the battlefield and learns of Goliath.
· 1 Samuel 17: 28-30 – Eliab chastises David for coming.

TWENTY-SIX

A SHEPHERD'S RESOLVE

"Some trust in chariots and some in horses,
but we trust in the name of the Lord our God."
—Psalm 20:7

Word of David's boldness spread through the camp and eventually reached the ears of King Saul as he sat brooding in his tent. The king's curiosity was piqued, but the mention of David, son of Jesse, from Bethlehem stirred something deeper: anger. Saul remembered the boy, the harp player who had fled the palace long before. Could it be that the same boy now dared to return, claiming he could defeat the Philistine champion? Summoning David to his tent, Saul prepared to put the impudent child in his place.

The king's tent was larger than most homes in Israel. The main room held not only a makeshift throne, but various tables, some with battle maps spread across them, others with platters of food. The room was dimly lit by a few torches as Saul's top advisors gathered in the shadowy corners, deep in conversation. Jonathan, the king's oldest son, was seated at one of the tables, intently scanning a scroll.

When David entered the tent, all conversations stopped as heads turned in his direction. Saul's gaze turned dark. The boy's youthful face, dusty and sunburned, betrayed no fear. His presence, unassuming yet confident, struck a strange chord in Saul's heart.

"So, it is you," Saul said, his tone sharp. "The boy who fled my court when I extended the honor of making you my armor bearer. And now you're here, claiming you can defeat the mighty Goliath? What makes you think you're anything more than a coward who abandoned his king?"

David bowed low, unflinching under the accusation of Saul's words. "My king, I did not leave out of cowardice. I left because the Lord called me back to my flock. He had lessons for me there that I could not learn in the palace. And now, He has called me here for this moment. The armies of Israel should not cower before this Philistine. The Lord is with us. Who can stand against the Lord?"

Saul leaned forward, his eyes narrowing. "You think the Lord sent you to fight my battles? You, a shepherd boy with no training and no experience? Do you know how many warriors have cowered at the feet of the mighty

Goliath? Tell me then, what makes you believe you can succeed where my greatest warriors would fail?"

David straightened, his gaze steady and unyielding. "My king, I have defeated a lion to protect my father's sheep. When the great beast took one of my lambs, I killed it and rescued the lamb from its jaws. The same God who delivered me then will deliver me from this Philistine."

Jonathan, watching from his seat, was surprised at the boldness of this young man. The shepherd spoke with such faith and certainty that Jonathan could not help but be drawn to him.

Saul laughed bitterly. "Really? You claim to have defeated a lion and now you think you can defeat a giant? Do you not see how absurd you sound?"

The advisors in the tent chuckled, their amusement a faint echo, but as Saul met David's eyes, his laughter faded. There was something there—an unwavering conviction, a calm certainty that defied reason. Saul's own faith had long been buried under doubt, but in this boy, he glimpsed a flicker of something he no longer understood. Once, I would have faced the giant without a second thought, he realized. The bitterness in his chest deepened.

"And if I send you to your death at the hands of Goliath?" Saul asked, his voice quieter now. "What then? Shall I bear the guilt of Israel being defeated by the Philistines?"

David's voice did not waver. "The battle is the Lord's,

my king. He has prepared me for this. I do not come with my own strength, but with His."

Saul leaned back, his fingers tapping the armrest of his chair as his attention turned inward.

Is this truly how my kingdom ends? Will I be remembered as the king who sent a shepherd to fight his battles? No, this cannot rest on me alone. I did what I thought was right; I fought for my people. And yet, Samuel cursed me, and the Lord turned away. His voice has been silent for so long. If the Lord wishes to use a shepherd to prove His will, then what choice do I have but to let it unfold? If the boy is victorious, I will be seen as the wise king who outsmarted the Philistines; if he fails, I can claim that the Lord is displeased with his people, not the king.

Saul studied the boy for a long moment before speaking.

"Very well," he said, waving dismissively. "Go, if you must. The Lord may yet find use for you where He no longer does for me. But if you insist on fighting, at least take my armor. Let's see how a shepherd fares as a soldier."

Turning to the side, Saul called over to the table in the corner, "Jonathan, bring my armor and help our champion prepare for battle."

Jonathan disappeared into another room before returning with the king's armor and placing it before David. David studied the armor cautiously. He ran his fingers over the polished metal, feeling its weight. The breastplate was too large, the sword too heavy.

As Jonathan helped lift and strap the armor in place, his curiosity about the shepherd increased. "Tell me David, where do you find such courage to fight this giant when every other man's heart fails them? Do you feel no fear?"

David was grateful to hear kindness in the voice of the king's son, something he had not felt in the tent so far. He turned his head and looked up to meet Jonathan's eyes. "Yes, I do have fear. I feel it fighting for a place in my heart right now as it has many times in my life. But I also have faith in the Lord and the promises He made to His people if we will listen to His voice. In this moment, all I can do is choose faith over fear, and pray for the strength to take another step forward."

Jonathan felt his own heart stirring within him as David's words filled him with hope and admiration. In David, he found something completely unexpected: a leader. Not a man with military experience or the strong and dominant personality of a ruler. This shepherd was the type of man he would follow into any battle. The type of leader Israel needed right now.

Jonathan finished buckling the armor and stepped away. David moved his arms around awkwardly and took a few unsteady steps before shaking his head.

Saul watched as the boy struggled, a bitter smile tugging at his lips. "It seems the Lord doesn't prepare everyone the same way," he muttered.

"My king," David said, removing the armor piece by piece. "I cannot wear these. The Lord has not prepared me with armor like this. Let me go as I am, with the tools He has given me."

Saul watched as David removed the armor and confidently picked up his staff and sling. There was no hesitation, no faltering and, against all logic, Saul too felt a sliver of hope flicker within him—though he quickly buried it under the cloak of his cynicism.

"Go, then," Saul said, his voice carrying a note of mocking finality. "And may the Lord be with you. What have I to lose? Perhaps you'll make a fool of yourself and die quickly. Either way, the Lord seems to have abandoned us already."

As David left the tent, the eyes of the soldiers followed him, their murmurs carrying a mix of disbelief and wonder. Despite his size and humble appearance, his boldness had earned their respect.

Jonathan felt the urge to run out of the tent and follow David, but decided it was better to stay, not wanting to appear disloyal to his father. Saul remained seated on the throne, his hands pressed together as he stared at the empty space where the shepherd had recently stood.

SCRIPTURES INFLUENCING THIS CHAPTER:

· 1 Samuel 17:31-37 – David volunteers to fight Goliath.
· 1 Samuel 17: 38-39 – David refuses Saul's armor.

CHAPTER

TWENTY-SEVEN

STONES BY A STREAM

*"You guide me with your counsel,
and afterward you will take me into glory."*
—Psalm 73:24

The camp was eerily silent as David stepped away to be by himself. The murmurs of soldiers faded behind him, replaced by the gentle rustling of leaves and the distant babble of water.

Before long, a stream came into view, winding its way through the valley. David paused by the water's edge, the words of Samuel, spoken long before, echoing in his mind: "You will gather your own stones along the path the Lord has set for you. Each one will carry a lesson, a strength you will need."

David knelt by the water's edge; the chill of the

stream felt refreshing as he washed his face. He reached into his shepherd's pouch, his fingers finding the stones that he kept separated from the rest. David closed his eyes, reflecting on the journey that had brought him to this point. After a few deep breaths, he began pulling them out, one by one.

The first stone he removed from the pouch was a dark red color with a translucent appearance in the sunlight. He knew this stone well for he had carried it the longest. It was the stone Samuel had given him on the day of his anointing. He had not understood then what it meant to be called by the Lord, but that vision had grown within him over time, just as Samuel had promised.

"This stone is for vision," David whispered. "When Samuel anointed me, I could not understand why the Lord would choose someone like me. I saw only a shepherd, the youngest in my family, unremarkable in every way. But Samuel and the Lord saw something greater—a future I could not yet imagine. Through both trials and victories, the Lord has opened my eyes to see beyond who I am to who I could become. My doubts and insecurities have been my greatest obstacles, blinding me to His plan. This stone reminds me to see beyond where I am and to trust in the potential He has placed within me. When we truly believe in what we can become, we start to become who we were meant to be."

He reverently washed the stone in the stream and placed it on the ground before him. He reached into his pouch for another, and he knew it instantly when he touched it. This was the stone he had collected the day he defeated the mighty lion. It was a dark brown color and not as smooth as the others. It reminded him of the moment when he had chosen to act instead of fleeing. He realized that on the day he defeated the lion, he wasn't much older or stronger than the times he had been paralyzed by fear. He had just made up his mind to be brave for one moment, and that one flash of bravery led to a heroic victory.

"This stone is for courage," he said, his voice steady. "For taking the first step, even when the outcome is uncertain. Sometimes the scariest step is the first one because the future is unknown, but nothing great can be accomplished if we never take the first step into that uncertainty. Courage is not the absence of fear; courage is deciding to act despite our fear."

He washed the second stone in the stream and placed it next to the first. "Vision and courage. Those two alone could defeat any enemy in life," he thought to himself.

The third stone he chose was slightly rough though weathered by time; he could feel its imperfections under his touch. As he lifted it from the pouch, he remembered the countless days tending sheep, the discipline it had required to wake early, to watch tirelessly, to care for the flock. It had not been glorious, but it had been necessary. His thoughts moved to the hours he spent learning from the craftsmen and Elders in town. All those little efforts multiplied over time had served as the foundation to prepare him for this day.

"This stone is for self-discipline," David reflected, remembering the day he had found it among the ruins of the stone wall. "Just as a capstone must rest on a strong foundation, greatness is built through patience, preparation, and faith in the process. This stone reminds me that true strength lies in the daily commitment to growth—doing what must be done, even when the task seems small. A meaningful life is not shaped by a single grand event, but by thousands of quiet acts of discipline and improvement. Mastery comes through consistency, and I must strive each day to become better than I was before, without thinking of recognition or reward. I am grateful to my past self for laying the foundation that brought me here, and I pray that I will always have the discipline to continue that journey. A true leader never stops growing, for without continual learning and self-reflection, even the strongest foundations can crumble—just like the wall where I found this stone."

Following the same process, David washed the grey stone and placed it with the other two. He studied them for a moment. "The vision to see where I'm going, the courage to step into the unknown, and the self-discipline to continue learning along the path. These are the attributes of a great and humble leader."

The fourth stone instantly brought with it a range of emotions. It was the polished black stone from Saul's palace. As he turned it over in his hands, David reflected on the many times he had been brought to the ground. His brothers' taunts, King Saul's scorn, and the lion's ferocity—each had knocked him down in their own way. Yet here he was, still standing, stronger than he was before.

"This stone is for perseverance," he said. "For enduring and pressing on when the road was long and the burden heavy. For getting back up when I was knocked down. For continuing when people mocked me. For surviving what life threw at me and still getting up the next day. This stone was ground down and polished over time by the loving hands of a craftsman before it could become the beautiful gem it is today. On this journey, some of my rough edges were smoothed away by the Master Craftsman as I have been shaped and strengthened by each setback I endured. Trials aren't meant to break us; they are meant to refine and polish us. Nothing can stop the person who refuses to give up."

He carefully placed the black stone with the others, beginning to feel the power of their combined lessons. Vision, Courage, Self-Discipline, and Perseverance.

As David contemplated the stones representing his journey, he had the feeling that one was missing, even though his pouch was now empty.

"One more," he thought. "I feel like there is one lesson that I've forgotten, something that ties them all together."

Kneeling by the stream, David said a prayer to the Lord, the One who had led him through his journey, the Master whose voice had been with him in both his victories and his defeats. "Help me," he pleaded.

He waited for the voice to come but was greeted only

by silence. The moment dragged on, yet he found that the silence did not disturb him as it would have in the past. In that silence, David found his answer.

His eyes remained closed as his hand plunged into the flowing water of the stream. He pulled up the first stone his hand touched. It was lighter than the others, almost delicate in its  simplicity. As his eyes opened, a rush of calming warmth coursed through his body. This was the stone he was meant to find.

"And this stone is for faith," David whispered. "For trusting in the Lord's plan, even when I cannot see the way, even when His voice seems silent. Without faith, all the lessons I have learned would be meaningless, for it is faith that binds them together. It is faith that turns vision into action, courage into strength, discipline into trans-formation, and perseverance into victory. Faith is the bridge between what is and what could be; the anchor that holds firm through every storm. If I lose faith in who I can become, then I will soon stop trying. Without faith in a larger plan, how would I ever hold on in the dark times? This stone reminds me that faith is the foundation upon which all else is built."

As he placed the light-colored stone with the others they seemed to hum in unison, giving off an unseen strength. David paused again to pray and give thanks to the Master, who had skillfully guided him to the precipice of his destiny.

He sat by the stream, lost in quiet reflection, until suddenly, the stillness was shattered by the pounding of the Philistine drums.

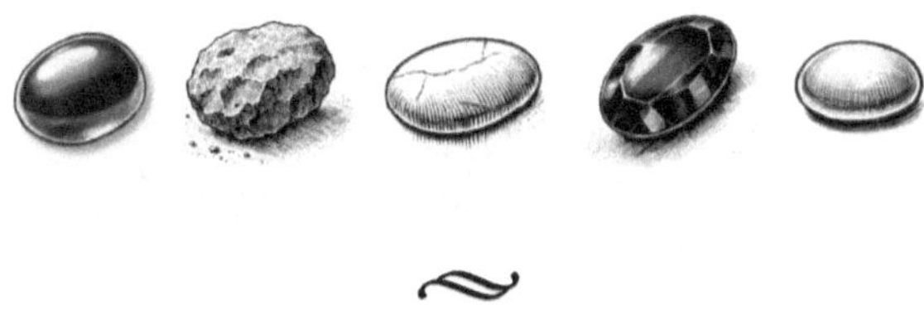

~

SCRIPTURES INFLUENCING THIS CHAPTER:

· 1 Samuel 17:40 – David and his five stones at the stream.

TWENTY-EIGHT

THE WALK TO DESTINY

"I keep my eyes always on the Lord.
With him at my right hand,
I will not be shaken."
—Psalm 16:8

David rose, placing the stones securely in his pouch one by one. Together, they were a reminder of everything he had learned and everything he had become. Vision, courage, self-discipline, perseverance, and faith—this was the ammunition he would take into battle with the giant.

The sun hung high in the sky as he reentered the camp, the eyes of the soldiers following him in silence. They still only saw a shepherd boy with a staff, a sling, and a few small stones, but David knew the truth: he was armed with far more than they could see.

The sound of the drums and yells from the Philistine camp echoed across the valley, a deep and unrelenting sound that seemed to pulse in time with the tension in the air. Goliath's voice followed, booming and taunting as it had every morning and afternoon for weeks.

"Is there no man among you who will face me?" he roared. "Will you cower forever in your tents? Send your champion and let us end this!"

The soldiers in the Israelite camp stirred uneasily, their eyes fixed on the ground. Some muttered under their breath, others stared out across the battlefield in shame. It was into this charged silence that David stepped.

As he walked toward the battlefront, the murmurs began. Then came the jeers.

"Is this a joke?" one soldier sneered. "They're sending a boy to lose the war for us. Where is our king?"

"We're finished," another muttered, shaking his head. "He'll panic and run before he even reaches Goliath."

Laughter rippled through the camp, bitter and mocking. David's steps did not falter. He kept his gaze forward, his heart steady despite the scorn that followed him. He pressed his pouch tightly against his side so he could feel the reassuring outline of the stones. He needed each of those lessons in this moment as much as in any other along his journey.

From the corner of his eye, he saw movement. King Saul emerged from his tent, his expression unreadable but his posture tense. He leaned against the entrance, his arms crossed as he watched David with a mix of amusement and disdain.

"So, this is our champion," Saul said under his breath, his tone dripping with sarcasm. "The shepherd boy who will win the day." He spat on the ground. "The Lord has left us to die."

As David passed, his steps steady and his head held high, Saul's chest tightened. I walked like that once, he thought bitterly. He clenched his fists, his nails digging into his palms. "The boy's faith will be his undoing," he muttered. "Do not expect the Lord's favor to last."

David didn't look back. He had determined that his best hope to survive this moment was to keep his eyes forward toward his goal. But as he approached the edge of the camp, he heard a familiar voice calling out behind him.

"David! Stop this madness!" It was Abinadab, his face pale with worry. "Turn back now before you bring shame on our family. This isn't your fight!"

"Listen to him," Shammah chimed in, his voice low but urgent. "You're going to get yourself killed, and for what? To be the fool who lost Israel to the Philistines?"

David paused, turning to face his brothers. His eyes, steady and bright, met theirs. "This is the Lord's battle," he said simply. "Not mine, not Israel's. The Lord will deliver us, as He always has."

"You arrogant child!" Eliab's voice rang out, sharp and angry. He stormed forward, his face twisted with fury.

"You think this is about faith? This is about war, David. Real men fighting real battles! You don't belong here. Go back to the sheep where you can't embarrass us any further. Our family will be shamed forever for this!"

David clenched his jaw, but he did not respond. Instead, he turned and continued walking, his pace measured and unyielding. Eliab's words followed him, but they could not stop him.

David didn't blame them; he knew his brothers' anger was rooted in fear, not faith. Of course, to them it would seem like madness to send the shepherd boy to battle. But they didn't know who he had become, and they had forgotten the promises made by the Lord.

"If the Lord is with us, who can stand against us?" he whispered to himself as he left his brothers behind.

As David walked forward through the last rows of soldiers, his eyes found one more familiar face. The king's son, Jonathan, was there at the head of a group of men. He said nothing, but gave David a reverent nod of encouragement.

David reached the edge of camp and paused, the enormity of the moment pressing upon him. This was the culmination of everything he had endured, the lessons learned through hardship, the effort poured into every small victory, the patience honed by countless quiet days in the hills, and the faith that had carried him through every trial. All of it had led him to this threshold, where a shepherd boy stood on the brink of destiny, prepared to confront the impossible with nothing but his faith and the stones in his pouch.

"Faith over fear. This battle belongs to the Lord," he whispered again, his voice too soft for anyone to hear. Then, with a deep breath, he stepped forward onto the battlefield.

TWENTY-NINE

FACING THE GIANT

"I sought the Lord, and he answered me;
he delivered me from all my fears."
—Psalm 34:4

Across the battlefield, Goliath squinted, his body stiffening as he took in the figure approaching him. A boy? Surely this was some sort of insult. No warrior's armor, no shield, just a sling and a stick. Goliath's lips curled in disdain, though the flicker of an unfamiliar feeling stirred within him. For years, his size and appearance had silenced any challengers before a battle could even begin. Yet now, here stood this boy, unarmed and unafraid, walking toward him with a boldness that felt almost otherworldly.

Goliath gritted his teeth, pushing the unease down. He raised his voice, determined to drown out the small, creeping doubt with noise and fury. If he could frighten the boy, he would win before the first strike.

"Am I a dog, that you come at me with sticks?" he bellowed, gesturing toward David's staff. The Philistines roared in laughter behind him.

David's pulse quickened. Seeking strength, he put a hand in his pouch and felt one of the stones. He knew which it was by its size and shape. He thought of Samuel, the oil of anointing, and the vision that had grown within him since that day.

"Vision," David said to himself, his steps unwavering. "The Lord saw in me what I could not see in myself. This Philistine makes the same mistake; he sees a child, but I am a king."

Goliath took another step forward, his laugh growing harsher. "Come closer, little boy. I will feed your flesh to the birds of the air and the beasts of the field!"

David felt the familiar sting of fear rise in his chest. He instinctively moved his fingers to another stone. It was larger than the first and he knew it immediately. He recalled the terror that gripped him when the lion charged, the way his hands trembled and his breath caught. Yet he also remembered the moment he chose to act despite his fear.

"Courage," David thought. "Courage is not the absence of fear, but the choice to act in spite of fear. The Lord delivered me then, and He will deliver me now."

Goliath snarled, raising his massive spear, and pointing it toward David. "Do you think you can defeat me with your childish games? Go back to your sheep, little shepherd. You have no place here. Find an opponent worthy of me!"

David's resolve was increasing as he moved forward, the giant's words having less effect on him. His hand found the third stone, the gray rock that represented the long days tending sheep, training with his sling, and learning from the wise men.

"Discipline," he reminded himself. "Every small moment on my journey has prepared me for this battle, I will not falter now. Step by step, a shepherd grows into a warrior."

The giant laughed again as he saw David continuing to move towards him. "You and your people are nothing but cowards. Your God is nothing. Come and face me if you dare and see how quickly I will crush you and your God beneath my feet!"

David's steps faltered for a fraction of a second, fear and doubt still battling to find a place within him. He pushed forward regardless, and his fingers found the fourth stone. He knew it was the black stone by its well-polished surface.

"Perseverance," David thought, his steps steady once more. "The road has been long and many times I wanted to quit, but after each fall, I got back up. The Lord has carried me through every trial and He will carry me through this one as well. I will not turn back now."

Goliath roared more loudly, hoping to cover up the growing uneasiness he felt about the unflinching determination of this boy. "Your God cannot save you, boy. Today, you will die by my hand, and Israel will fall! There is no hope, only death!"

David knew which stone he would find next even before his hand discovered it: it was the smallest and lightest of them all, but also the most beautiful. He thought of the small voice that had been his constant guide, illuminating his path through every shadowed moment: the Master's voice. It was the voice that knew the beginning from the end, that spoke with a wisdom far beyond his understanding, and that always asked him to trust in the Lord's plan even when he couldn't see the next step forward. This was the stone that tied them all together.

"This last stone is for faith," David whispered. "I have faith in the Master's plan and in his timing. I believe the words He has spoken to me and I know this battle belongs to Him. He has never failed me, and He will not fail me now."

With that, David began to run. His feet pounded the earth, his heart racing as he closed the distance between himself and the giant. Goliath's eyes widened in surprise at the sight of the boy charging toward him.

As the distance to the giant closed, David dropped his staff and pulled the sling from his belt. But, reaching back into his pouch, he was startled when his fingers found **only a single, unfamiliar stone.**

Confusion.

Fear.

Doubt.

They all tried to rise up within him, but there was no time for such things; no time to wonder what had happened.

The moment of destiny had arrived, and he only had one shot to take.

Keeping his eyes focused on Goliath, he placed the new stone in his sling. He began swinging it over his head, the rhythmic hum filling the air, growing faster and sharper with every rotation.

Ahead, Goliath's voice thundered one final taunt: "Now you die!" he roared, lifting his massive spear and planting his feet in a battle stance.

David maintained his focus and resolve as he came within range. His heart was beating loudly in his chest yet, in the final seconds, a surprising sense of calm flooded his body. This was what his entire journey had prepared him for. Every lesson, every failure, every act of faith had shaped him into who he was. This was not just a single moment in a battle; it was the culmination of all he had learned and all he had become. He was not merely facing Goliath; he was confronting every fear, every doubt, every obstacle he had ever known or would ever face in his life. David was made for this moment, and this moment was made for him.

David released the stone.

It flew through the air, slicing with an almost supernatural precision, as though guided by an unseen hand. For a heartbeat, the valley seemed to hold its breath. Silence descended as every eye was fixed on the scene before them.

With a crack loud enough to be heard by both armies, the stone struck Goliath squarely in the forehead, just below the edge of his massive helmet, embedding itself deeply in his skull as though destined for that very spot.

The giant's mocking laughter choked into silence; his expression frozen in stunned disbelief. Slowly, his massive frame began to sway, the sheer weight of his armor amplifying his fall. Then, with an earth-shaking thud, Goliath crashed to the ground, his immense shadow vanishing beneath him as dust rose into the air like a final breath.

THE VALLEY WAS STILL as David lowered his sling, his breath coming in sharp, shallow bursts. The soldiers on both sides stared in shock and disbelief, their eyes fixed on the impossible scene they had witnessed.

"How could this happen?" they all wondered.

The answer lay not in the stone or the sling but in the unseen power that guided it—a power greater than any man, greater than the giant who now lay silent upon the earth.

"The battle belongs to the Lord," David said softly

again. "When a willing heart aligns with divine purpose, the extraordinary becomes possible."

The silence in the valley seemed to stretch for eternity before it was broken by a single cry from the Israelite side. It was Jonathan, who, without realizing it, had followed David part way onto the battlefield, drawn by the pull of the moment and a power he could not fully understand.

"Goliath has fallen!" he screamed victoriously.

A roar erupted as the Israelite soldiers surged forward, their weapons raised in triumph. The Philistines hesitated for a moment before panic set in, and they began to retreat. The once-mighty army fled, their confidence shattered with the fall of their champion, as the armies of Israel raced across the valley in pursuit.

David stood motionless, watching as the chaos unfolded around him, his heart pounding with the enormity of what had just transpired. As his mind replayed the final scene of his battle, his hand darted into his shepherd's pouch, certain to find it empty. Instead, to his surprise, his hand closed around **five familiar stones**, their surfaces unmistakable.

SCRIPTURES INFLUENCING THIS CHAPTER:

· 1 Samuel 17:41-48 – David advances despite Goliath's taunts.

· 1 Samuel 17:49-51 – David defeats Goliath with a single stone.

· 1 Samuel 17:52 – The Israelite army chases and defeats the Philistines.

THIRTY

AFTERMATH

"Come and see what God has done,
his awesome deeds for mankind!"
—Psalm 66:5

As the day drew to a close and the battlefield quieted, David was summoned once again to the tent of King Saul. Throngs of soldiers crowded around him, congratulating him and cheering his name as he made his way to the king's tent. Sitting on the throne, Saul's expression was unreadable as he studied the young shepherd standing before him, sweat and dust streaking his face. Goliath's massive sword, far too large for David to wield, was strapped across his back as a trophy of the impossible victory.

"You've done what no man in Israel dared to do," Saul said, his tone a mixture of disbelief and grudging respect. "Tell me, boy, how did you bring down the giant?"

David bowed his head briefly. "The Lord delivered Goliath into my hands, as He has done with every challenge I've faced. I just needed to believe in His promises."

"That's it?" Saul responded with a mocking chuckle. "The Lord just delivered the victory to you?"

David didn't flinch; his confidence unshaken. "The entire army of Israel was focused on the size of the giant, I decided to focus on the size of the Lord. He is more powerful than any giant, no matter how strong or ferocious they are. And as long as I believe that in my heart, there is no challenge I cannot conquer with Him by my side."

From outside the tent, the sounds of celebration grew louder as the soldiers recounted the events of the day. It came as no surprise that David's name was being cheered far more than the king's, and hearing it tore Saul apart inside.

Saul studied David in silence as the undeniable truth settled over him. This boy—this man—truly was the one the Lord had chosen to replace him. A hollow feeling crept through him, confirmation of what he had feared all along. From the moment Samuel had spoken of another, Saul had known his days were numbered. He had begun to sense a threat in every whisper, a challenger waiting in every shadow, and now the moment had come.

His lips curled into a faint, bitter smile. "The small boy with the harp that fled my palace all those years ago. I should have trusted my instincts then," he thought to himself. He studied David now, standing tall despite his youth, the marks of battle still fresh on his brow. The Lord's favor was evident, radiating from him in a way Saul had not felt in years.

The sting of it pierced deeper than Saul expected. He had once been where David now stood, full of promise, anointed by the prophet, his faith unshakable. He too had been called by the Lord and entrusted with the fate of Israel. Yet somewhere along the way, his faith in the Lord had faltered as it gave way to pride in his own strength.

Saul's remorse was brief, being quickly replaced by a renewed sense of determination. Although his past failures were undeniable, so too was his current position. He was still the king and until it was taken from him, the crown still rested on his head.

Saul straightened, his fingers tightening on the armrests of his chair. If the Lord had abandoned him, then he would hold his kingdom together by sheer will. He had risen by his own might once before, and he could do it again.

Saul dismissed everyone from the tent. He rose and paced back and forth in silence for what seemed like an endless few moments.

"Don't you see, David?" Saul said with a sneer. "The Lord may have chosen you, but I am still king. I may have fallen from His favor, as Samuel claims, but this throne is mine. Power does not rest on faith alone. It rests on strength—on control. And that, I still have."

Saul moved closer, his eyes narrowing as he studied David's face. "You may carry the Lord's blessing today, but let me tell you something, shepherd—blessings are fleeting. When the weight of the crown presses down on you, when the people look to you for answers you do not have, you will see how fragile it is. And when it falters, when you are left with nothing but the expectations of men and the silence of heaven, you will understand what it is to stand alone."

David said nothing, his expression steady, though Saul could see the fire in his eyes—the faith that Saul had once carried and lost. It burned brightly in the young man, unshaken by the king's bitterness. It both angered Saul and pained him in equal measure.

Saul returned to his chair, the tension in his shoulders easing into a weary resignation. "Go, then," he said, his voice quieter now. "Take your victories. Take what the Lord has given you. But know this, David: I will not give up my throne. I have fought too hard and bled too much to see it slip away without a fight."

David bowed his head slightly and, without a word, he turned and walked away, leaving Saul alone in the dim light of the tent. The king sat motionless, staring once again at the empty space where David had stood. In that moment, Saul fully understood his place—not as the

Lord's anointed, but as a man desperately clinging to a crown that no longer belonged to him.

DAVID'S BROTHERS found him as he made his way through the crowd of soldiers congratulating him. Eliab was the first to speak, his voice low and strained. "I didn't think you could do it," he admitted. "I was wrong."

David met his brother's gaze, searching for sincerity. "I didn't do it myself, the Lord was with me," he replied simply.

Eliab hesitated then nodded humbly. "I have treated you so poorly. I was jealous that you were the one being called to greatness and afraid that I was being left behind. I am sorry."

David couldn't stop the tears from forming in his eyes at the sincerity of Eliab's words.

Abinadab and Shammah said little, their expressions torn between amazement and lingering disbelief. Though they congratulated him, David could feel the unspoken words hovering in the air.

He looked at them lovingly and spoke. "I know it was hard to believe that the youngest and smallest among us would be chosen for this. Your resentment is understandable, it took me a long time to believe it myself. I'm learning that the Lord often brings about his greatest works through the smallest and simplest of means. The past can remain in the past. Let us go forward together from here and see what the Lord has prepared for us."

They embraced as brothers, for the first time that any of them could remember, before joining the soldiers celebrating around them.

SCRIPTURES INFLUENCING THIS CHAPTER:

· 1 Samuel 17:57 – David brought before Saul again.
· 1 Samuel 18:8-9 – Saul becomes jealous of David.

THIRTY-ONE

STONES BY THE FIRE

"I waited patiently for the Lord;
he turned to me and heard my cry...
He put a new song in my mouth,
a hymn of praise to our God."
—Psalm 40:1, 3

That night, as the camp settled, David sat alone by the fire, his thoughts turning inward. In front of him, on the ground, lay his five stones, their surfaces reflecting the light of the fire. He looked at them one by one: vision, courage, discipline, perseverance, and faith—each had given him strength as he approached Goliath, and each would guide him in the battles yet to come. Yet in the final moment, they had somehow all disappeared. He couldn't fully comprehend it although he knew it had to be something divine.

As David stared into the fire, lost in thought, the sound of footsteps broke the stillness. He looked up to see an old man approaching. David recognized the figure immediately, illuminated by the flickering flames. The prophet's presence brought with it a sense of calm and purpose.

"You have walked a long road in a few short years, David." Samuel said, settling onto a rock across from him. "And yet, your journey is only beginning."

David nodded, looking into Samuel's eyes for the first time in what seemed like ages. "I didn't understand it at first," he admitted. "When you called me, I was certain you had made a mistake. I couldn't see how someone small and timid like me could ever become a king."

Samuel's eyes softened. "If I remember correctly, the word you used to describe yourself was 'nobody'. Fortunately, the Lord sees what we cannot. He saw the heart of a king in you long before your victory today. My role was simply to listen and obey, as was yours. Your journey began with a single choice—to answer the call—and was strengthened by your growing belief in the Lord's plan. The more you learned to listen to His voice and follow its promptings, the more prepared you became for this moment. One day, people will ask how you won this battle. Tell them the truth: 'I did not win it that day. I won it in every unseen moment that led me there.'"

David's gaze dropped to the stones in front of him. He

reached down and picked one up, holding it out to Samuel. "This belongs to you," David said, his voice low. "You gave it to me when I thought I would never be more than a shepherd, to remind me of the vision the Lord had for me. I don't need it anymore; the vision is clear now."

Samuel leaned forward, studying the familiar stone he had carried from his youth. After some reflection, he gently pushed David's hand back toward him. "No, David. This stone is not mine to take. It was never meant to stay with me. You will need it still, perhaps even more now than before. The vision may be clear today, but there will be days when doubt clouds your sight and the path ahead feels uncertain. When that time comes, let this stone be a light in the darkness of doubt."

David looked down at the stone, its smooth, red surface feeling warm in his hand, and then back at Samuel. "Thank you," he said quietly, his voice filled with emotion. "I will keep it with me always."

The prophet smiled faintly. "It is not me you should thank, but the Lord. I merely listened to His voice. And so have you, David. That is why you succeeded today, not by your strength, but by your faithfulness."

David glanced at the other stones and back to Samuel. "Today, in the moment just before defeating Goliath, I reached into my pouch to grab one of these five stones, but they were gone. There was just one stone, different from any of these. That was the stone that brought down the giant. I don't know how to explain or understand what happened.

Samuel studied the stones, considering David's words. "The Lord's ways are not our ways and at times it is hard for us to understand why He does things. But it seems there may be a lesson to be learned from that stone. As you've pondered it, what are your thoughts?"

David sat in quiet contemplation before answering. "Leading up to the battle, I was wondering which stone I should choose first to defeat Goliath and which I would use next if that one missed. I tried to decide which was the better shape but soon moved onto which represented the most important principle. In the end, I couldn't choose one and so I decided to let the Lord decide for me."

Samuel let a faint smile cross his lips. "I think maybe you've already found your answer."

As he pondered Samuel's words, a flash of inspiration came to David's mind. There wasn't just one stone that could have defeated Goliath, it took the power of all of them. The principles he had learned along his journey were not strong enough on their own; the power came when they were united in purpose. His vision had guided him. His courage had moved him. His discipline had honed him. His persistence had sustained him. And his faith had brought him to the point of victory. These were more than just stones in his pouch; they were the foundation of who he had become. The Lord had brought them together for the defining moment when David would need them all to achieve what he was destined for.

As David sat, lost in the wonder of this realization, Samuel rose to leave. "Take time to enjoy today's victory,

David. You have accomplished a great feat and saved your people the same way you saved your flock in the past. Your journey is not over and the path moving forward will not be easy, there are still giants to defeat, but the same God who delivered you today will walk with you every step of the way."

David rose and they embraced in silence. In that sacred moment they both remembered their first meeting; when a prophet and a shepherd met on a hillside, each one seeking answers for the journey the Lord had put before them.

Moments later, David watched Samuel disappear into the darkness as quietly as he had come. The old prophet was right, this was only the beginning. The road ahead would be long and fraught with challenges greater than Goliath. Yet, for the first time, David felt ready to face them all.

The End

EPILOGUE

In the vast night sky overhead, the stars glimmered —unchanged from those countless nights David spent alone with his flock. But on this night, they shone down on the future king of Israel, as a reminder of the Lord's infinitely unfolding plan.

Centuries later, those same stars would cast their glow upon another sacred night, where shepherds in Bethlehem—watching over their flocks on the same hills David once walked—would be the first to receive the news: a child was born, a descendant of David, not in a palace but in a humble manger, coming not to claim a throne of earth, but to bring peace to a broken world. As David had once risen from a shepherd to a king, so too would this child rise—not to rule a nation, but to redeem all mankind.

And though David could not have known it that night, his victory was but the first note in a symphony of redemption, a melody that still plays in the hearts of those who believe. For the battle always belongs to the Lord. And in His hands, even the meekest of people and smallest of stones can change the course of history.

Luke 2:4-21

CONTINUE THE JOURNEY...

REFLECTIONS ON THE FIVE STONES

The story of David and Goliath is one that echoes through the ages—a shepherd boy who faced an unbeatable foe with nothing but a sling, a few stones, and unwavering faith. But what lies beneath the surface of this tale is more than just a victory over a giant; it is a journey of growth, transformation, and purpose.

Each of the five stones David carried into the battle was more than a weapon. They were symbols of the principles that had shaped and prepared him for this defining moment. Together, they tell a story of how small, deliberate lessons forge a path to greatness.

The same principles David learned on his journey can help each of us on our own path as we look to slay the giants in our life. His stones can be ours. His journey, a mirror. Just like David, we are all being shaped for something greater still.

Let's take a moment to dive deeper into each of the 5 stones and learn how they can make an impact in your life today.

THE FIRST STONE: VISION

David's journey began with a vision. When Samuel anointed him, David could never have imagined the path that lay ahead. He saw only the hills of Bethlehem, the flock he tended, and the quiet life he thought he could never escape. When David's vision was thus limited, the thought of accomplishing anything greater was nearly impossible. But once he began to believe in what was possible for his life, his entire story changed.

The first stone reminds us to see beyond our current circumstances and believe that we were put on this earth for a greater purpose. A clear vision of where we are going changes the ordinary into the extraordinary; obstacles transform into opportunities and learning experiences on our journey toward what we are meant to become.

How do you find your meaning?

Here are some questions you could ask yourself:

- What makes you the happiest?
- What are you naturally good at?
- What do people often compliment you for?
- When are you at your very best?

Reflecting on these questions can help you identify and unlock the natural talents and abilities you were sent to earth with. They are clues pointing to your divine purpose and will help you share the best version of yourself with the world.

THE SECOND STONE: COURAGE

Courage was the spark that turned indecision into action. The difference between David's previous encounters with the lion and with his victory came down to one moment of bravery, the courage to do something rather than just watch and hope. As David's journey progressed, he learned that courage is not the absence of fear but the decision to act in spite of fear.

Often, we know what we want to become, and we may even know how to do it, but fear of the unknown keeps us paralyzed in our familiar situation, leaving our dreams to wither away over time. This stone teaches us that the first step is often the hardest, but it is also the most important because without taking that first scary step into the unknown, we will never enjoy the beautiful journeys life puts before us.

Questions to reflect on:

- If you could move forward without fear, what would you do differently in your life?
- How would your life look if you acted that way?
- What "first step" have you been avoiding because it feels too uncertain?

Answering these questions can link your courage to your vision. Once you've defined who you want to become all you need is the courage to get started.

Remember, the obstacles we are avoiding or the steps we are afraid to take never end up being as bad as we imagined them to be. Convince yourself to be brave for just one moment at a time and watch how the world begins to open up for you.

THE THIRD STONE: SELF-DISCIPLINE

In the quiet countryside of Bethlehem, David learned the value of discipline. Day after day, he tended his flock, protecting them from danger, guiding them to safety, and caring for their needs. These seemingly mundane tasks prepared him for far greater responsibilities. As David learned from the village Elder: "If you try to place the capstone without working on the foundation, everything will crumble."

People often praise the accomplishments of great men and women, but they rarely see or recognize the days, months, or even years of dedication it took to reach those achievements.

Building the foundation is never glamorous, but it is necessary. Nobody becomes great overnight and nothing meaningful is built in a day. Discipline is the foundation upon which greatness is built, and this stone reminds us that faithfulness in small things paves the way for the larger victories in life.

Questions to reflect on:

- What daily habits or disciplines are helping you grow into the person you want to become?
- Is there an area where you need more consistency before expecting greater rewards?
- What is one step you can take this week to strengthen your foundation for future success?

Never underestimate the power of small and consistent improvement. Decide what kind of life you want to build for yourself and who you want to become then start laying the stones of your foundation. It may seem slow or go unnoticed at first, but it will show up with major victories in the long run.

THE FOURTH STONE: PERSEVERANCE

David's life was not without failure. He stumbled, he doubted, and he faced ridicule from those closest to him. Yet he rose each time, learning and growing with every step. Persistence and perseverance carried him through the valleys of doubt and despair, teaching him that the path to victory is rarely straight or easy.

Life is designed to challenge us because that is the only way we can grow into our potential. If nothing presses against us, we will never gain the strength to raise the banner of victory. This stone is a call to keep going, to rise again and again, no matter how many times we fall. The Lord doesn't waste the stumbles, He uses them to teach us how to run. Every time you get back up, you have gained a victory.

Questions to reflect on:

- Do you believe that the challenges you face have a purpose? Why or why not?
- Can you recall a time when failure taught you something valuable? How did it shape you?
- What is one failure in your life that you need to reframe as a lesson rather than a defeat?

Life is going to knock you down sometimes and the path you plan for yourself will fall apart. That is just how it goes. But make a promise to yourself that you will always get back up and keep trying. You don't fail, you learn. And when you get back up, you'll be stronger than you were before. When the next trial comes your way, you will be even more prepared to overcome it and keep moving forward.

THE FIFTH STONE: FAITH

The final stone was the most powerful of all. Faith was the thread that wove all the lessons together. It was faith that guided David's vision, strengthened his courage, sustained his discipline, and fueled his persistence.

Faith sustains us through hard times and gives us a reason to keep going. Faith reminds us that our battles belong to the Lord and that our role is to trust in Him, act boldly, and let Him do the rest. He has a grand plan for each of us and when we start to believe in His promises, we can become who we were meant to be. Faith is believing that wherever you are right now is exactly where you are supposed to be.

Questions to reflect on:

- Are there areas where you struggle to trust in God's plan? What holds you back?
- What is one situation in your life where you need to step forward in faith rather than fear?
- How can you strengthen your faith in times of uncertainty or hardship?

Sometimes in life you see your path clearly and it is easy to follow, but sometimes it is obscured. In those moments you need to hold onto the faith that there is a plan for you and that you will never be abandoned. The sun will still rise tomorrow, and you will rise with it.

FINDING YOUR STONES

David's victory over Goliath was not just about a single moment on the battlefield. It was the culmination of a life shaped by these principles. And while this part of the story ends with the miraculous defeat of a giant, the lessons it teaches continue to resonate through to us today.

We all face giants in our lives—challenges that seem insurmountable and obstacles that test our resolve. But like David, we carry stones in our pouch, lessons learned through trials and triumphs, times of failure and of faith. When the time comes to face our giants, it is not the sling or the stone that ensures victory, but the character forged by the journey.

The battle belongs to the Lord, but the preparation belongs to us. And with vision, courage, discipline, perseverance, and faith, there is no giant too great, no obstacle too daunting, and no calling beyond our reach.

What stones are you already carrying? What lesson is life teaching you right now that will serve as the foundation for your battles ahead? The journey to greatness is not just in the size of the battles you face, but in the strength and character you build along the way.

There is a beautiful future waiting for you, one filled with both trials and triumphs, giants to be defeated and crowns to be claimed. **Your stones are waiting, what will you do with them?**

About the Author

Kris Heap is a lifelong seeker of wisdom and a master storyteller whose journey has traversed the professional world, personal development, and spiritual mentorship. A compelling speaker and writer, Kris brings to life ancient truths through modern eyes, blending scripture, symbolism, and soul-stirring narrative.

With a heart rooted in faith and a passion for helping others overcome life's giants, Kris wrote *The 5 Stones of David* not just as a retelling of a familiar story, but as a guide for personal transformation. His desire is to help readers discover their own stones for success and fulfillment so they can walk confidently into the battles of everyday life.

Kris serves his community as a healthcare provider, humanitarian, and religious leader. He is a husband, a father, and a man who believes that the smallest moments—if met with faith—can change the course of history.

Kris is available for speaking engagements, workshops, and podcast interviews. To learn more, visit **www.krisheap.com**, or follow him on social media **@krisheap**.